P9-CRR-511

"I'm innocent."

Gage watched her features tighten as he explained that he'd been framed for murder. "I think it goes back to the explosion in Lab 7. Something happened there, but I don't know what. You have to believe me."

It was asking a lot, after what he'd put her through. But he thought he saw the stark lines of her face soften, just a little. If he could hold her in his arms, connect with her and help her remember what they meant to each other, he could get her on his side. But before he could move, someone knocked on the door. "Police."

Gage took in her suddenly fixed gaze and rigid posture, and thought she was calculating her chances of making a run for it.

"You'd better get out of here," Lily said, her voice high and thin.

"It's not that easy. They'll have the front and back doors covered." With time running out, Gage made a life-and-death decision. And prayed he wouldn't live to regret it.

He was kidnapping his own wife.

Dear Reader,

Writing *Chain Reaction* has been the culmination of a very exciting experience for me. It's the first book in a miniseries called SECURITY BREACH. The other two books are *Critical Exposure* by Ann Voss Peterson and *Triggered Response* by Patricia Rosemoor, respectively.

You may remember that Patricia, Ann and I have written several three-in-one Harlequin Intrigue books—three novellas in one book. This time we got the chance to expand our canvas with a three-book miniseries. And we hope we've brought the same kind of larger-than-life characters and exciting plots to these three novels.

We've set the story in one of my favorite locales—Maryland's picturesque Eastern Shore and the Baltimore area.

The explosive beginning of the miniseries takes place in Lab 7 at a company called Cranesbrook. My hero, Gage Darnell, is caught in a lab accident. When he wakes up in Beech Grove, a private mental hospital, he tries to figure out why he's being held captive and why nobody will give him any information. Escape seems to be his only option, but once he breaks out, he's in even deeper trouble. And the worst part is that he drags his estranged wife, Lily, into danger with him.

The other two exciting stories in the miniseries continue with the characters you meet in *Chain Reaction,* starting with Rand McClellan, the police detective charged with hunting down murder suspect Gage Darnell.

Enjoy!

Sincerely,

Ruth Glick writing as Rebecca York

REBECCA YORK

RUTH GLICK WRITING AS REBECCA YORK

CHAIN

REACTION

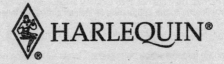

HARLEQUIN®

TORONTO • NEW YORK • LONDON
AMSTERDAM • PARIS • SYDNEY • HAMBURG
STOCKHOLM • ATHENS • TOKYO • MILAN • MADRID
PRAGUE • WARSAW • BUDAPEST • AUCKLAND

If you purchased this book without a cover you should be aware
that this book is stolen property. It was reported as "unsold and
destroyed" to the publisher, and neither the author nor the
publisher has received any payment for this "stripped book."

ISBN-13: 978-0-373-88720-0
ISBN-10:   0-373-88720-5

CHAIN REACTION

Copyright © 2006 by Ruth Glick

All rights reserved. Except for use in any review, the reproduction or
utilization of this work in whole or in part in any form by any electronic,
mechanical or other means, now known or hereafter invented, including
xerography, photocopying and recording, or in any information storage
or retrieval system, is forbidden without the written permission of the
publisher, Harlequin Enterprises Limited, 225 Duncan Mill Road,
Don Mills, Ontario, Canada M3B 3K9.

All characters in this book have no existence outside the imagination of
the author and have no relation whatsoever to anyone bearing the same
name or names. They are not even distantly inspired by any individual
known or unknown to the author, and all incidents are pure invention.

This edition published by arrangement with Harlequin Books S.A.

® and TM are trademarks of the publisher. Trademarks indicated with
® are registered in the United States Patent and Trademark Office, the
Canadian Trade Marks Office and in other countries.

www.eHarlequin.com

Printed in U.S.A.

ABOUT THE AUTHOR

Award-winning, bestselling novelist Ruth Glick, who writes as Rebecca York, is the author of close to eighty books, including her popular 43 LIGHT STREET series for Harlequin Intrigue. Ruth says she has the best job in the world. Not only does she get paid for telling stories, she's also the author of twelve cookbooks. Ruth and her husband, Norman, travel frequently, researching locales for her novels and searching out new dishes for her cookbooks.

Books by Rebecca York

Don't miss any of our special offers. Write to us at the following address for information on our newest releases.

Harlequin Reader Service
U.S.: 3010 Walden Ave., P.O. Box 1325, Buffalo, NY 14269
Canadian: P.O. Box 609, Fort Erie, Ont. L2A 5X3

CAST OF CHARACTERS

Gage Darnell—What turned him from law-abiding citizen to criminal on the run?

Lily Darnell—Did she and her husband have a future together?

Randall (Rand) McClellan—Could this police detective figure out who murdered Tucker Hillman?

Brayden (Bray) Sloane—Why did he disappear?

Sidney (Sid) Edmonston—Did the Cranesbrook president have something to hide?

Nelson Ulrich—What kind of experiments was he conducting in Lab 7?

Wes Vanderhoven—Was he really in the same fix as Gage?

Richard Francis—Could he and his partner solve their murder case before it was too late?

Officer Maxine (Maxie) Wallace—Could she supply Rand and Richard with vital information?

Hank Riddell—What was he hiding from the police?

Dr. Frederick Morton—Was he paid off to hold Gage captive?

Evan Buckley—Was he working for Gage or against him?

Chapter One

"Gage Darnell, you...you low-down liar. If you don't come home today, don't bother!"

Glad that he wasn't standing face to face with his wife, Gage clenched his large hand around the telephone receiver. But he had no trouble picturing the anger flashing in Lily's beautiful green eyes. Or her blond hair swirling in a golden cloud as she shook her head. She probably had a pot of chili on the stove. And crisp clean sheets on the king-size bed, since this would have been the first time in weeks that they'd seen each other.

He'd been aching to make love with her, then eat the wonderful meal she'd prepared while they caught up on the details of each other's lives. And he'd hoped he could still make it home—at least for one night before he had to go back to work.

That was before two of his security men had called in sick, and he'd decided he had to stay on the Eastern Shore. He hadn't felt comfortable dumping the total responsibility for the Cranesbrook detail on Brayden Sloane. Not when his partner was already jumpy and out of sorts.

So Gage was still two hours away from home, where Lily was expecting him to walk in the door any minute. He'd figured they could talk about Five Star's problems after dinner. Now he was trapped in a no-win situation, caught between his wife and his partner.

He owed them both his loyalty, but his relationship with Bray went all the way back to when they'd been in Special Forces training together. Then, in Afghanistan, when they'd saved each other's lives, the bond had grown even stronger.

He gulped and said, "Something's come up, and I can't leave Cranesbrook."

"I arranged to take off work this weekend. I thought you did, too. What's going on now?"

While he tried to frame an answer, she plowed ahead. "You're saying Cranesbrook Associates is more important that our marriage?"

He recognized the calm, deliberate tone. It was a dangerous sign.

"Sweetheart, I'm under contract to protect this place." The rest of it was too complicated to explain in a five-minute phone conversation, so he fell back on one of his tried-and-true arguments. "And you know we need the money."

As soon as the words were out of his mouth, he realized he'd made a big mistake.

Her voice turned cold and hard as she answered. "Gage, we don't need the money. We both have good jobs. Our finances are just fine. Or they would be—if you didn't buy all that electronics equipment every time you got some spare cash."

"It's all stuff I need for my—"

"Experiments," she finished for him. "If you're not at Cranesbrook, you're in your garage workshop. Or your home gym pumping iron."

As he realized how far off track they'd gotten in a few short minutes, he winced. He didn't bother to defend his need to keep in shape. But he couldn't stop himself from saying, "I'm on the edge of a breakthrough with the miniature advance warning system."

"How many times have I heard that?"

He'd been on the defensive. Now he was starting to get pissed off.

"If I can perfect the electronics, we never have to worry about money again."

"Gage, don't you understand…"

Before she could finish the sentence, alarm bells began to clang in the security station and somewhere else on the Cranesbrook campus. His gaze shot to the monitoring panel he'd installed in the lounge area. Either they had a false alarm—or an emergency in Lab 7.

Lily obviously heard the noise. "Good God. What was that?"

"Don't know. Gotta go."

On alert, yet relieved to end the conversation, he slammed the receiver into the cradle and ran into the hall, where he almost collided with Bray, who was ushering office workers toward the exit.

On the second day of their deployment to Afghanistan, Bray had saved Gage's life by yanking him in back of a cement wall just as a sniper had opened fire on their patrol. And he'd done the same favor a few months later for Bray, pulling him out of a burning truck that was about to explode.

They had both come home with all their body parts intact, thanks in part to their good working relationship. Until lately the only problem was Bray's tendency to go by the book while Gage was more impulsive. That had led to more than a few arguments about how to run Five Star Security.

The security work had been pretty routine up till now. Suddenly this was like being back in a war zone, with crazed civilians getting in the way of split-second decisions.

"It's Lab 7," Gage shouted to Bray as he helped a panicked-looking secretary into the grassy area in front of the administration building.

When she grabbed his arm, he gently detached himself. "You'll be fine, ma'am."

Turning to his partner, Gage asked, "Was there an intrusion at the gatehouse?"

"Not according to the sensors."

As they exchanged information, they moved away from the crowd of administrative staff and lab workers who were already milling around in the park along the shore of the small, artificial lake. Too bad the alarm hadn't gone off forty minutes later when most of the civilians would have been gone for the day.

Evan Buckley and Pete Westerly, the two other men on guard duty that afternoon, were also outside in the fall sunshine, herding people toward the parking lot. Buckley looked around and saw Gage, then turned quickly back to his duties. The two of them weren't on the best of terms, but at the moment the guy looked as though he was doing his job.

Like Gage and Bray, the other security men were clad in khaki uniforms that set them apart from the lab staff and the office workers.

"Put the vehicles between the people and the

buildings," Gage shouted as he headed toward the laboratory. "But don't let anyone leave until we check this out."

As he closed in on the main operations building, Gage unholstered his weapon.

"What do you think? Malfunction or an intruder?" Bray asked.

"I hope it's a malfunction."

When they saw Sid Edmonston charging toward them, they exchanged a quick look.

Just what they needed. Cranesbrook had facilities up and down the East Coast, principally in New Jersey. Usually the company president wasn't on site down here, but he'd arrived a couple of days ago for some meetings with both his lab and office staff.

Under the best of conditions, the tall, lanky executive was a pain in the ass. In an emergency, he was going to be impossible. According to rumors, this division of the business still wasn't paying its way, and Edmonston had made it clear that he was going to close the labs down if he didn't start seeing results.

"What happened?" he demanded, shouting over the sound of the clanging bell. A thin layer of perspiration glistened on the bald dome of his large head. And from the way his narrow-eyed stare focused on his security guards, it looked as if he was holding them personally responsible for the emergency.

"We're about to find out," Gage answered, keeping his voice even.

"This is a security violation," the president barked, confirming Gage's assessment that the man was looking for someone to blame.

He bit back a sharp retort, but Bray wasn't able to keep his annoyance to himself. "How the hell do you know what happened?" he demanded. "It could just be someone setting off the alarm by accident."

Yeah, and carpets can fly, Gage thought, but he didn't bother to correct his partner, not when he knew Bray was likely to get into a shouting match with the company president.

Edmonston glared at them. "Get in there and find out what's going on."

"We're on it, if you'll allow us to proceed," Gage said, making an effort to keep his voice mild as he walked to the keypad in the entryway and punched in this week's number code.

To his relief, the earsplitting alarm stopped. At least the system wasn't shorted out.

Before they could get inside, Nelson Ulrich came pounding toward them. Apparently he'd been with the other employees in the parking lot, but he'd no doubt shoved his way through the crowd and come charging back to make sure his precious lab wasn't in danger. He might be the Director of Research, but Gage had seen him working late at night and assumed he was deep into some kind of experiment of his own.

If Edmonston was a pain in the ass, Ulrich was worse. Whatever he was working on, he'd been acting as if it was his last chance for greatness. Gage and Bray had been making bets on whether the research genius would have a heart attack or a stroke before he brought the project in.

"Make sure nobody's gotten to my computer or my notes," he shouted.

"You got it," Bray agreed.

Ulrich looked as if he was going to follow them into the lab.

"Step back," Gage ordered. To his relief, the two men moved away from the doorway. "And don't come in until we give you the all clear." That last part should have been unnecessary, but he knew that both these guys needed the reminder.

As Bray opened the door, he and Gage slipped back into combat mode. Instead of automatic rifles they held side arms as they entered the small foyer, which had been designed to impress the casual visitor. The floor was quarry tile, the walls were rich cherrywood, and the doors leading into the individual labs were stainless steel. They'd both wondered if some of this money might not have been better spent on an increased security force and some better equipment.

This afternoon, the opulence was marred by the sight of a man's body sprawled near the entrance to one of the labs.

Blood had poured from a wound on the back of his dark head and dripped onto the tile floor. But head wounds always made an impressive mess, even when they were superficial.

Because Gage was closer to the guy, he hurried to the man's side and turned him over. It was Dr. Martin Kelso, one of the company managers. His eyes were closed, his rounded face was pale, and he lay absolutely still.

"Martin?" Gage asked.

He didn't answer, didn't move.

"What's he doing here?" Bray asked, echoing Gage's own thought.

"Hell if I know." He felt the man's neck and was relieved to find his skin warm and his pulse beating steadily. "You get him out. I'll check the labs," Gage told his partner.

"Right." Bray was already pulling out his cell phone to call for medical assistance.

Gage stood and caught a flash of movement to his left. Whirling with his gun pointed toward the intruder, he saw his own reflection in one of the polished metal doors that lined the room.

He looked tall and lean—and grim-faced. A man with a military-short haircut and an automatic weapon in his hand. Lucky he hadn't put a couple of slugs into the metal panel. Edmonston would probably have charged him for the damage.

Alert for trouble, he pulled open the door to his left, then stepped cautiously into Lab 7, his gaze sweeping the twenty-foot-long room. The lab rats in their cages were squeaking and running around, probably set in motion by the alarm bell. But they still hadn't quieted down now that the noise had stopped. Probably the monkeys down the hall were even more alarmed.

Gage saw no intruders, but his view was blocked by the long lab tables, granite-topped with cabinets below.

Most of the work area was tidy, but the light was on in one of the wall-mounted hoods designed to protect lab personnel from dangerous chemicals. Either someone had been interrupted in the middle of a procedure or an intruder had been messing with an experiment in progress.

As Gage crossed the room, he spotted a pair of

trouser-clad legs on the floor, sticking out from behind the lab table closest to the hood.

Whoever was there lay deadly still. Was he hurt? Or was this an elaborate setup for an ambush?

Gage crept cautiously toward the lab table, then rounded the corner in one smooth motion, gun pointed at the man on the tile floor. This time he didn't have to roll the victim over. The guy lay on his back, and Gage saw it was Wes Vanderhoven, one of the lab technicians.

"Wes?"

The man didn't answer. But he was obviously breathing. Thank God.

To Gage's right, a closet door stood ajar. If there was an intruder in the lab, the assailant could be inside, waiting to take him down, too.

Keeping his eyes on the closet, he ducked low and ran across the room. Before he reached the doorway, an explosion shook the room.

He sprang back, hoping to take cover on the other side of the lab table, but he was already too late. Smoke came shooting out from behind the closet door as though someone had set off a defective firework cone.

"What the hell?"

The smoke geysered up and out, filling the room with a curtain of thick, choking fumes.

Coughing, Gage backed away, wishing he had a radio headset like when they'd been in the military. But Sid Edmonston had vetoed that item in the Cranesbrook contract because he hadn't wanted any transmission in the lab area.

Then someone moved up beside him. Even with smoke pouring into the room, he saw it was Bray.

"What the hell do you think is going on?" Gage managed to gasp, his throat burning.

When his partner didn't answer, Gage turned his head, seeing Bray frozen to the spot.

"Bray?"

"Okay, okay."

But his friend didn't seem okay. He was staring straight ahead, his body taut, reminding Gage of that day in Afghanistan when Taureen Morgan had stepped on the landmine and gotten blown apart right in front of Bray's eyes.

As Gage wondered what the hell he was going to do, Bray snapped back into action. "Maybe we should beat a retreat with Vanderhoven."

In unison, they moved back toward the man on the floor. But now Gage couldn't even see the lab technician in the thickening atmosphere.

"Where is he?" Bray choked out.

"Hell if I know." Dropping to his knees, Gage crawled across the floor, looking for the man.

Maybe that maneuver saved his life. He was at ground level when the closet door blew off and flew across the room. A shock wave rolled toward him, and he ducked back around the table. Pieces of ceiling tile rained down around him, and a heavy light fixture landed inches from his head.

With the rain of debris came more smoke, billowing out to envelop the room. Flames flickered inside the closet. In the seconds before the explosion, he'd lost track of Bray. In the next heartbeat, he almost lost track of himself. The choking atmosphere in the lab hit him like a cloud of drugged smoke from an opium den. Within seconds, his head felt like it was filling with cotton batten and he fought a wave of nausea.

The smoke was clogging his lungs, turning his thoughts to oatmeal, but his training pushed him forward.

When the debris stopped falling, the lab was deathly quiet. The rats had stopped squeaking, and he wondered if they were dead or just unconscious now.

He made a heroic effort to crawl toward the door, but he got only a few yards farther before he felt his arms and legs begin to quiver. Desperately, he flailed out a hand and caught the leg of a lab stool. It was hot, and he pulled his hand back, just before the stool tipped over and crashed to the floor near his head.

He cursed as it hit the cement surface, then lost the battle to keep down his lunch. Vomit spewed out in front of him, and he realized he was crawling through it as he tried to reach what he thought was the door—if he hadn't gotten turned around in the smoke and fire.

He felt as though he was battling to push his way through a sea of glue. He was still fighting to escape from the lab when everything went black.

LILY DARNELL spoke desperately into the cell phone she was holding. "Gage, oh Lord, Gage. Call me as soon as you can. Tell me what's happening. I'm using my cell to keep the house line clear."

She clicked the End button, then paced to the window and stared out at the trees that hemmed in the backyard on three sides.

She had been fighting with Gage only minutes earlier. Well, not exactly fighting. She'd been mad enough to spit nails, and he'd been keeping his famous cool. Then an alarm bell had rung, and he'd dashed off into who knew what kind of danger.

She waited two minutes, feeling the tension in her neck and shoulders increase. Finally, she dialed the main Cranesbrook number again—and got the same infuriating female voice.

"We're sorry that our St. Stephens facility is currently closed. Our regular hours of operation are Monday through Friday, 8:30 a.m. to 4:30 p.m. If you would like to leave a message for the administrative staff, please press 1 now. If you would like to contact our laboratory complex, you must know your party's extension."

There was no mention of the security men, but Lily pressed the extension for Gage's private line. Once again his crisply recorded message said, "This is Gage Darnell. Leave a message and J'** get back to you as soon as I can."

She'd already done that. And he hadn't called back. When she'd heard the clanging in the background, she'd hoped it was some kind of false alarm.

Now…

She stared out at the backyard of the eighty-year-old house they'd bought in Baltimore County when they'd moved down here from Philadelphia three years ago.

Gage had loved the super-size lot because it gave them privacy, and the detached garage where he could work on the electronics projects that he thought would bring him financial independence.

She hadn't loved moving to Baltimore, but

she'd understood her husband's arguments that the Philadelphia market was saturated with security companies, and he'd have a better chance of establishing his business farther south.

All she'd realistically required was a drive to work that was under a half hour and a decent kitchen where she could test some recipes she wanted to try at Chez Amelia. She'd gotten both.

Her sister, Pam, was already in the area. And Lily had made some women friends among the staff at the restaurant. Sometimes they went shopping or to the movies together. But that didn't make up for having her husband absent most of the time. She was beginning to wonder if she was going to end up like the rest of his family—out of sight and out of mind.

For a split second she thought about calling Pam. But she didn't want to let on how worried she was. Instead, she grabbed the remote and turned on the television, standing across the room as she clicked through the local channels, looking for some kind of news report. Nobody was deviating from their regular programing.

Which was good, she told herself. If the media hadn't swarmed to Cranesbrook, everything was okay.

Still, her legs felt shaky. Dropping into Gage's

easy chair, she closed her eyes, struggling for calm. But she couldn't convince herself that staying here and waiting for her husband's call was the right thing to do.

She had to go down to St. Stephens. Of course, Gage wouldn't appreciate having her hovering around. But that was too bad. She was worried, and she couldn't just sit around waiting for him to remember that he had a wife at home who might be concerned about the abrupt way their phone conversation had ended.

She grabbed a light jacket and was halfway out the door when the phone rang.

She said a little prayer of thanks. Gage had remembered he had a wife who might be worried about him, and he was calling back to tell her what had happened. As soon as she knew he was okay, she was going to light into him for scaring her spitless.

Snatching up the phone, she said his name in a rush of pent-up anxiety. "Gage?"

"Mrs. Darnell?"

It wasn't him. "Yes," she answered, preparing to get this guy off the line as soon as possible so her husband could call.

"This is Sidney Edmonston."

She'd met the Cranesbrook president when

she'd gone down for the Christmas party last year. He'd been pleasant in a distant sort of way. Now he was calling her on the phone, and she was sure he didn't have good news.

"Is Gage all right?" she asked, aware of the gasping quality of her own voice. "I was just talking to him, and I heard an alarm ring."

The man's voice was grave, warning her that something bad was coming. "I'm afraid there's been an accident."

Fear slammed into her, physically knocking her backward. Fear and guilt. "Where is Gage? Is he all right?" she managed to ask.

Edmonston made an exasperated sound. "I don't have much information. He's been taken to Cambridge General Hospital."

"When?"

"A half hour ago."

"I'm on my way down."

Chapter Two

Gage was dreaming about his first date with Lily, when he'd decided that a guy whose mother worked as a maid didn't have a chance with a woman whose family was the cream of Philadelphia society. That was before he'd realized she didn't give a damn about all that upper-crust stuff.

But when he reached to pull her close, she vanished. He was confused. Then he realized he'd been dreaming, and the sound of murmured voices had wakened him.

His eyes blinked open, then promptly closed as bright light hit them.

"He's back again," a man's voice observed. The words were accompanied by the smell of peppermint on the guy's breath.

Again. Back again. When was the last time he'd been awake? He had dim memories of coming to in an emergency room. Of nurses and doctors

frantically rushing around. He'd told them he was
fine. He'd tried to climb off the table, and
someone had pushed him back and jabbed a
needle in his arm.

He'd come to the next time in a hospital room
and smelled peppermint. When?

He felt limp and weak, as if he'd been lying
flat on his back for days, but that couldn't be
true. Could it?

More scenes slithered through his mind. He'd
been yelling. Demanding that they turn him loose.
Telling them they had no right to keep him
confined. Then...

He tried to block the next part out. But the
toxic memories rushed back. He'd been out of
control. Fighting to get away from hands that
held him down.

But now he was back to normal. Well, not exactly
normal, although he was feeling a lot calmer.

"Where am I?" he asked. His voice hoarse, as
though he'd been screaming and hurt his throat.

"In the hospital." He knew the man's soothing
tone was meant to reassure him. It had the
opposite effect.

A cold chill danced up his spine. When he tried
to sit up, something kept him from moving.
Slitting his eyes, he saw that his wrists were re-

strained to metal bars on the side of the bed. As if he was a nut case or something.

In a calm voice, he made what sounded like a reasonable request. "Let me up."

"You need to rest. Everything's all right."

Gage took a deep breath, ordering himself not to panic, searching for calm inside himself as he tried to focus on the man who was speaking.

"What hospital is this?" he asked.

"Beech Grove."

The name meant nothing. He kept his gaze on the man standing over his bed. He was medium height with thinning blond hair, and he was wearing a white coat and a calculating expression that didn't match his calm voice.

"Who are you?"

"Dr. Morton."

A woman in a white uniform stood beside him. She was taller and more muscular than the doctor. Her brown hair was cropped short. Steel-rimmed glasses accentuated the harsh lines of her face. Although she was dressed like a nurse, her aggressive stance made her look more like a nightclub bouncer confronting an unruly patron.

An old movie flashed into his mind—*One Flew over the Cuckoo's Nest.*

Thinking of that story made the back of his

neck tingle. The nurse—Nurse Ratched—had been the tinhorn god ruling a ward in a mental hospital. The one who ordered shock treatments and lobotomies for the men who got out of line.

Lord, no!

He wanted to believe that this was a regular hospital and that he was recovering from…from what?

His mind supplied an answer: the effects of an accident at the Cranesbrook labs.

But if this was a medical facility, why wasn't the doctor checking his vital signs or something?

He struggled to breathe slowly and evenly, to convince the two people standing over him that he wasn't going to start screaming or fighting again. It wasn't easy to come across as normal—not when he was lying here trussed up like a pig ready for slaughter.

"Dr. Morton and Nurse…?" he inquired politely.

"Nurse Dumont," she supplied.

He nodded. Then said, "I want to see Lily."

"She's not here," the doctor answered.

She hadn't come down to St. Stephens? He couldn't believe that. They might have been fighting when all hell had broken loose in Lab 7. But she'd be worried.

All hell?

He tried to grab on to that memory—and succeeded in capturing an impression of a body lying on the floor. Then a loud bang followed by smoke.

Or had he dreamed all that? Like he'd been dreaming about Lily.

He didn't know. The lack of information and the restraints on his wrists pushed his frustration level almost beyond endurance. But his instincts were good. He was sure it would be a mistake to let Dr. Morton and Nurse Dumont know that he was getting agitated.

Luckily they didn't have him hooked up to a bunch of machines so they couldn't know how hard his heart was thumping inside his chest.

He searched his mind for a reasonable topic of conversation under the circumstances and came back to Lily. "I'd like to see my wife," he murmured.

"Visitors would not be good for you at this time."

"How long have I been here?"

"That's not important," the doctor answered with maddening calm.

If Gage could have moved, he would have surged off the bed, slammed the doctor and nurse into each other and made a run for the door.

But the restraints kept him where he was.

He flexed his muscles. They felt spongy. Even

if he were free to stand, his knees might buckle under the weight of his own body.

Making deliberate eye contact with the physician and keeping his voice under control, he said, "I think I have a right to know what's going on."

Dr. Morton chose to look away. "We'll talk later," he muttered, then gave a small, dismissive wave of his arm to Nurse Dumont.

It must have been a signal, because she stepped smartly forward. When she bent over Gage, he saw a hypodermic in her hand.

"Wait!" he shouted.

Ignoring the protest, she jammed the needle into his upper arm.

"You need to sleep," the doctor added.

Gage didn't need to sleep. He needed answers. And he needed to get away from this bed, from this room. But the medication made him woozy. Pulse pounding, he tried to fight it, but the effort was wasted.

The last thing he remembered was the smell of peppermint wafting toward him.

SOMETIME LATER, voices woke him again.

He took a cautious breath, searching for the telltale essence of peppermint. He didn't detect it. The doctor must not be in the room. Or maybe he'd switched to lemon drops, because now that scent hung in the air.

Two women were talking. As he listened, he lay still, breathing evenly with his eyes closed.

"Let me show you how we take care of him." That was Nurse Dumont.

Skilled hands touched his body, and he forced himself to lie still.

"I haven't handled a restrained patient before. Is it safe to be here?" a trembly voice asked. It belonged to a woman who was apparently learning the ropes from the master.

"He's still out, and the restraints will keep him from hurting you or himself, while we bathe him."

"Okay."

Gage was glad of the warning. He lay passively on the bed as they gave him a sponge bath. In truth, it felt good to have the perspiration washed off his body.

Ms. Lemon apparently couldn't keep her mouth shut. As she worked, she said, "I guess you want him all nice and clean for Dr. Morton."

"Yes. He's with Vanderhoven now."

"I heard that there was another security guy caught in the explosion. Brayden Sloane. But he disappeared after the accident."

"Where did you hear that?" Nurse Dumont asked sharply.

"Around town. People talk, you know."

"What else are they saying?"

"Nothing much. Security is very tight at Cranesbrook."

Good thing they weren't taking Gage's pulse, because his heart was thumping now. He willed it to slow and was surprised that the maneuver seemed to work.

"Sorry. I guess I'm a little nervous," the rookie nurse apologized.

"You'll get the hang of it."

"Should we shave him?"

"I did that last time. We don't need to do it every time we bathe him."

Finally the two women left him on the bed, still held in place by wrist restraints. His head was muzzy, and he wanted to drift into the safety of sleep again. But he knew it was only a false refuge. When he woke up again, he'd still be in this bed. And still be a prisoner.

The question was—why were they holding him? Did he know too much? About what? Or had someone set him up?

He recognized the last question as paranoid. Yet he couldn't shake the notion. He'd had a couple of run-ins with one of his guards. Evan Buckley. He'd caught the guy asleep at his post one evening. And another time Buckley had been breaking one of Five Star's standing rules about talking on a cell phone while on duty.

Gage had been on the verge of firing the guy.

Could Buckley have had the guts to cook up a nasty surprise for Five Star management? Maybe he'd been ticked off enough to do it. But then what? Was he paying Dr. Morton to keep him here?

It sounded pretty far-fetched. But far-fetched was the best Gage had at the moment.

He clenched his fists. His nails needed clipping, and the pain helped him focus his resolve. He would get out of here.

But how?

LILY WAS barely aware of the heat and swirling activity in the sleek, stainless-steel restaurant kitchen. The charged atmosphere wasn't unusual for a Baltimore hot spot at dinner. But this was lunchtime, and she had been called in for a double shift because Chez Amelia had a big birthday celebration in one of its private rooms.

She should be cooking three orders of veal medallions. Instead, she stared down at the oversize skillet, her vision turned inward.

She ached to drive back to the Eastern Shore so she could be near Gage. When she'd arrived at Cambridge General Hospital, Gage wasn't there, and nobody would tell her where he was. In a panic, she'd driven to the Cranesbrook campus and found it locked up tighter than Fort Detrick, the army biological testing lab.

Then she'd been startled to find the man at the gatehouse wearing gray pants and a blue shirt with an Ace Security patch on the left shoulder.

"Did you fire Five Star?" she asked when she'd been escorted to Sid Edmonston's plush office.

"Your husband is out of commission, and Sloane is missing. I needed to get somebody in on short notice," the company president told her. "Sorry I had to make that decision, but we've got a situation here."

He went on to give her the bad news about Gage. Not long after arriving at the emergency room, her husband had turned violent. They'd sedated him and moved him from the medical facility to a private mental hospital called Beech Grove.

She drove directly from Cranesbrook to Beech Grove. But the physician in charge, a Dr. Morton, refused to let her see Gage because he was under sedation. Praying something would change, she rented a motel room for the night and came back the next morning, then sat in the waiting room for hours. Finally, at the end of the day, Dr. Morton told her Gage wasn't responding to treatment. According to the doctor, Gage was either violent or out of it and it would be dangerous for her to see him, so she might as well go home and wait for news.

As it turned out, she had no choice. The imperious Amelia St. James told her that, if she wanted to keep her position, she'd better report to the kitchen for the dinner shift on Monday.

She was tempted to tell her boss to take the job and stick it—until her saner side prevailed. Five Star Security had been kicked off their biggest account. Peggy Olson, who ran the office in Baltimore, had frantically switched the Cranesbrook men to other duties, including installing security systems.

Without the Cranesbrook account, cash was tight at the company. To keep from being a drain on Five Star resources, she needed to keep her job, unless she wanted to borrow money from her parents. And she was damned if she'd give them the satisfaction of saying, "I told you so."

That was why she'd dragged herself to Chez Amelia and spent the past two evenings and this afternoon trying to focus on such vital matters as perfectly prepared bearnaise sauce, wild mushrooms and herbed risotto.

Ordinarily, she took pride in her work. She knew her parents had been upset when she'd chosen culinary school over college. But she'd selected the best, the CIA, the Culinary Institute of America.

Like Gage, she was ambitious. She wanted to open her own restaurant, although there was no way she could afford that yet.

But work wasn't her biggest priority. That was her marriage. Or it had been—until Gage had started treating her like an appendage to his real life.

She'd hoped she could get their relationship back on track. Now...

The smell of browning butter made her snatch the skillet off the burner. She'd come within a few seconds of ruining some very expensive meat, and she looked around to see if anybody else in the kitchen was watching.

Sue Carmichael gave her a sympathetic smile. She was Lily's best friend at work, and Lily had talked to her about the accident at Cranesbrook. But there was no chance of talking now. They were both too busy for conversations.

Maybe in a few hours she could call Beech Grove again. Not that she expected the staff to tell her anything.

She was starting to think she needed a lawyer.

Could a lawyer make the mental hospital tell her anything besides "Mr. Darnell is not responding to treatment"?

After transferring the veal to three plates, she passed them to one of the line cooks to add the potatoes au gratin, Swiss chard and garnish.

Moisture blurred her vision, and she blinked. If she'd been alone, she would have lowered her head to her hands and given in to the need to sob out her frustration—and her guilt. She'd give anything if her last words to Gage hadn't been angry. She'd give anything to hear him reassure her that he hadn't been distracted, that he hadn't been focused on their angry exchange when he should have been thinking about business.

No, scratch that last thought, she told herself. Gage was a professional. He would have snapped back into soldier mode as soon as he had to respond to an emergency. She had to keep believing that or she'd come apart at the seams.

WHEN THE nurses left, Gage slitted his eyes and studied the room, looking for an escape route. In case someone was watching, he barely moved his head as he looked around. There were two doors. One led to the hall, the other to a bathroom. Did it have a window he could squeeze through?

Not unless he got out of the damn arm restraints.

When he heard footsteps in the hall, he closed his eyes again and forced his facial muscles to relax.

The smell of peppermint wafted toward him, and he knew Dr. Morton was back.

The little man crossed to him and shook his shoulder. "Mr. Darnell?"

He pretended he was coming out of a fog. "Yes?"

"How are you feeling?" the doctor asked, his voice hearty. Nurse Dumont was standing right behind him.

"Better. Could you loosen my wrists and crank my bed up?"

"Not a good idea."

Gage struggled not to grit his teeth. "If you think I'm crazy, give me a sanity hearing."

"Now, now, don't be hasty," Morton said, as though he were talking to a naughty child. "You'd be a danger to yourself if you were allowed your freedom."

"Why?"

"You and some others were exposed to a dangerous chemical."

"What chemical?"

"Something they were testing at Cranesbrook."

"What is it supposed to do?"

"That's proprietary information. We're going to

keep you here for observation until we find out how it affected you."

"And I can't see my wife?"

"I'm afraid not."

"What about my partner? Bray."

"He's not available."

Because he escaped? Gage didn't want to give away that he'd picked up that piece of information earlier when the nurses were talking. Instead, he strove for sincerity when he said, "I want to cooperate with you."

"That's good. We've lowered your dose of medication. I think we can have a more productive conversation in a few hours."

The doctor started toward the door.

"Wait!"

"Just rest now. I'll be back in a few hours," Morton said firmly. Nurse Dumont followed him out of the room.

Alone again, Gage lay on the bed, his breath shallow.

Rest! That's all he'd been doing in this damn place.

Feeling more clearheaded by the moment, he looked around the room again, taking in additional details. The one window was covered by bars. He had to assume it would be the same in the bathroom.

The walls were an institutional green. Besides the bed, there was no other furniture, not even a chair or a television set bolted to the wall. Instead there was a video camera.

He was under surveillance.

Straining his ears, he listened for sounds around him. Now that the doctor and nurse were gone, he felt like the only human being for miles around, although he knew that couldn't be true. Lord, what if they just left him here tied to the bed? He wouldn't put it past that bastard Morton.

The thought made his heart pound. They wouldn't tell him how long he'd been here or when he might be discharged. They wouldn't even let him out of bed. Not good.

His eyes were drawn to the cuffs on his wrists.

They were made of some sort of soft material on the outside, with a padded interior, designed to inflict minimal damage on his flesh, he supposed. Probably because Morton didn't want any evidence to show on the body.

Gage swore under his breath, wondering again if he was suffering from paranoia. Was that from the chemical he'd been exposed to?

Again he focused on the cuffs that prevented his hands from moving.

Lord, what if Lily saw him this way? He'd

longed for her, but the idea of her finding him trussed up like a mad dog made his insides curdle.

"Lily." He whispered her name. They'd had such a close, warm relationship when they'd first married three years ago. He'd been thrilled that a beautiful, giving, creative woman like her was interested in a hard-bitten soldier like him. Not just a soldier. A guy who was way below her in social status. When she'd agreed to marry him, he'd vowed to make their marriage work.

She was the most creative person he had ever met. She could turn a pound of ground beef into food fit for a king. And she'd made a beautiful home for him, using more imagination than money, since he hadn't let her take any gifts from her snooty parents. The way she could turn a garage-sale castoff into a thing of beauty never failed to amaze him. Like the old mantel that she'd made into a headboard for their bed.

And in bed...they had mind-blowing sex. He'd never known how good making love could be until he'd fallen in love with Lily.

He went into a little fantasy, thinking about what he wanted to do when he held his wife in his arms again. He'd been stuck at Cranesbrook for weeks, and they'd planned a weekend focused on each other. Then, at the last minute, he'd had to cancel out on her.

What a fool thing to do. He should have told Bray he was going home and slotted Evan Buckley for extra work. Only he'd been afraid Buckley would screw up.

Instead of second-guessing his decisions, he pulled his mind away from his present circumstances. Closing his eyes, he imagined himself and Lily in their king-size bed. A bed big enough to roll around in and have some fun.

They were both naked, and Lily was lying on top of him, her body pressed provocatively to his, all her familiar curves teasing his nerve endings, her lips brushing back and forth across his. He wrapped his arms around her, pressing her close, reveling in the taste of her, the touch of her fingers on his face.

She moved against his erection, and he dragged in a shuddering breath.

Lord, he would explode if she didn't take him inside her, then give him a view of her beautiful body as she sat up and began to move.

Her eyes sparkled as she grinned down at him, and he grinned back, knowing they were on the same wavelength.

The heated images had him hard as a stovepipe.

When he tried to move his hands, the restraints snapped him out of the fantasy. He was in a hospital bed, with his wrists cuffed to the rails. Not at home in his king-size bed with his wife. And it was dangerous to escape into his imagination. The more he tuned out the real world, the less likely it was that he could change his actual situation.

Clenching his teeth, he struggled to bring his mind back into safer territory. But he couldn't stop thinking about his wife.

She had given him so much. And he hadn't believed he deserved any of it. He'd been so determined not to be like his father, who had never been able to support his family. But *her* family was part of it, too. He'd wanted them to know that she hadn't made a mistake by marrying a guy without a college education. A guy who'd fiddled around with electronics since he was a kid, then learned more in the army. He'd been proud of his skills. Too proud, apparently. Because now he understood that he'd been proving his in-laws right all along.

He'd neglected his wife—the flesh-and-blood woman—and gone into overdrive with his career, so he could feel as if he was doing right by her. She'd wanted to have a baby. He'd said they had to wait until they were financially secure.

Now, deep down, he knew he'd been too focused on success. Had he gone so far that he'd ruined their marriage?

He felt moisture gathering behind his eyes, and he fought back the tears. Hell, he couldn't even wipe them away if they dribbled down his cheeks. And the idea of the surveillance camera picking up *that* made his gut twist.

Hating his own weakness, he fought off the attack of maudlin emotion by grabbing for his anger. He might have made mistakes in the past, but he hadn't gotten himself into this fix. Someone had put him here.

"This is your wake-up call," he muttered to himself. "You have to get back to Lily and tell her how much you love her, how much you appreciate her. How much you need her."

But how could he, when he was in this damn bed, cuffed to the handrails?

He ached to break free of the restraints so he could wrap his arms around his wife and make up for all the times he'd neglected her. And as that need took hold, he discovered something interesting. The restraints around his wrists weren't as tight as he'd thought. It appeared that the straps hadn't been fitted securely through the buckles. Somebody had screwed up. Maybe little Nurse Lemon.

Whoever had made the mistake, he fully intended to take advantage of that oversight.

As he wiggled his hands, the restraints loosened even more. He focused on his right wrist, moving his arm as much as he could, giving himself more leverage. After several minutes, the strap gave, and he was able to pull his right hand free.

Feeling like a kid who'd gotten caught cheating on a test, he moved his arm under the covers, then glanced toward the video camera, expecting Nurse Dumont and a burly orderly to come charging through the door.

But nobody came. Either the monitor wasn't attended at the moment, or the person watching wasn't doing his job.

Whichever it was, maybe the patient had a chance to get away.

Gage reached to unbuckle the other cuff. The effort left him breathing hard, but he wasn't going to rest until he got out of this place or died trying.

The last thought made his skin prickle. Cautiously, he pushed himself up, fighting a wave of nausea. When it passed, he worked the mechanism on the bed that lowered the bars on the right side.

After swinging his legs over the edge, he eased himself to the floor, where he stood holding on to the bed frame and feeling like an eighty-year-old man instead of only thirty-two.

How long had he been here anyway?

He was sick and shaky, and unable to rid himself of the feeling that he'd lost a big chunk of time. They'd been drugging the rational thought out of him. Now Dr. Morton wanted to talk to him so he'd eased up on the medication. How long before the doctor came back? And what about the video camera? Did someone already know he was out of bed? His only choice was to assume he was still in the clear.

Still, he hated to operate blind and with no plans. Unfortunately, all he could do was wing it, because staying under the control of these people wasn't an option.

He stopped for a minute, considering everything that he remembered so far.

If he was in a loony bin maybe there was something seriously wrong with him, and they were trying to cure him. He rejected that theory immediately. He was thinking straight, now that they'd eased up on the meds. But if he really was okay, why was he here? And if he was crazy, wouldn't he feel perfectly okay? Did most psychotics think they were just peachy, or did they know something was wrong?

When the circular reasoning gave him a headache, he stopped trying to figure it out. Maybe if he could talk to Vanderhoven, that might help clarify the situation. And maybe they could help each other get out of this place.

He tottered to the window and peered out. He was at the back of the building, where he saw thick woods. On the day of the lab explosion, the leaves on the trees had been green, even though it was the beginning of October. They were still green on most of the trees, which meant that not too much time must have passed.

Not as much as a week, he hoped.

After doing a few stretches and some deep knee bends to limber up his arms and legs, he crossed to the door and tried the knob. It was locked. Damn!

Now what? His longing for escape made him focus on the lock. Was there anything he could use as a pick? He looked around, seeing nothing useful in the room. Frustrated, he twisted the knob again and heard a click.

Maybe he'd been wrong, and it hadn't actually been locked. Maybe he'd been too weak to open it on the first try.

Or was this a setup? Did they want him to try to escape so they'd have an excuse for…what? Getting rid of him permanently?

If that were true, he was playing right into their hands. Still, this might be his only chance to make a run for it.

Cautiously, he cracked the door and looked out. The room was one of several along a hallway. He waited and listened.

About thirty feet away he saw a man and woman standing with their backs to him and talking. The woman was Nurse Dumont. And even from the back, he knew the man was Hank Riddell. Son of a bitch.

Riddell was a creepy little PhD who was always sucking up to the senior researchers at Cranesbrook. So, had they sent him here to keep tabs on Gage? And probably on Wes Vanderhoven, too.

While Gage was considering his next move, he caught a lucky break. Riddell and Dumont turned and walked down a side hall.

Gage heard a door slam. Maybe they were going to check on Vanderhoven. Or have a look at the monitor displaying the scene from Gage's room.

Which they'd find was now empty.

Gage was barefoot and still wearing the hospital gown. But since this might be his only chance to escape, he walked quickly down the hall.

As he rounded the corner, his plans changed abruptly when he almost tripped over an older man swishing a wet mop across the tile floor.

Chapter Three

The man froze in mid-stroke, a look of surprise and horror on his face. Obviously, he didn't expect an escaped mental patient to step around the corner.

His gaze darted to the wall and Gage saw what he'd given away. Within reach was a box that looked like a fire alarm.

When Gage leaped forward, the man defended himself, raising his mop and swinging it like a baseball bat, sending dirty water spraying onto the wall. Gage's reflexes were still way below his usual standards, but he managed to duck awkwardly, then go on the attack.

The man was a maintenance worker, not a trained fighter. And he wasn't very strong, either. Thank God.

They both slipped on the wet floor like a couple of circus clowns executing a crowd-pleasing routine. They went down with Gage on top.

Somehow he was able to land a blow on the man's chin. Then another.

"Sorry," he muttered as his opponent went limp.

The whole incident had taken less than a minute.

Expecting guards to swarm down the hall or Nurse Dumont and Hank Riddell to come charging back, Gage raised his head and looked wildly around. But nobody came to the maintenance man's rescue.

Leaping up, Gage ran toward the nearest door. It was locked. So was the next one, and he felt panic rising in his chest. The third knob turned, and he found himself staring into a large utility closet with cleaning products and rags arranged neatly on shelves around the walls.

Jackpot!

He dashed back to the man on the floor and saw his name was embroidered on his uniform shirt.

"Tucker."

First or last name, he wondered as he caught the man's limp body under the arms and dragged him inside the closet.

After he'd hidden the guy, he went back for the telltale mop and bucket. There was nothing he could do about the wet floor.

Sweat had broken out on his body. Ignoring the clammy sensation, he turned on the light, then quickly stripped off the guy's shoes, slacks and shirt, leaving him with his shorts and sleeveless undershirt.

Knowing that every second he stayed here brought him closer to capture, Gage discarded the hospital gown, then pulled on the shirt and pants.

There was no rope on the shelves, but he used several long rags to tie the man's hands and feet and to gag him.

Before he finished, Tucker was already stirring, and Gage worked faster.

The man's eyes blinked open. For a moment he looked confused, then he focused on Gage and made a mumbled sound. When he kicked out, Gage jumped back.

"Sorry to leave you here, but somebody should come looking for you soon."

Gage pulled on the man's tennis shoes. They were a size too big, which he figured was better than too small.

Somebody had left an Orioles baseball cap on one of the shelves, and he put it on, pulling the bill low over his face.

He opened the door again and scanned the hall, wishing he had some kind of weapon. No, scratch that last thought. If he had a weapon, that would give Morton an excuse to shoot him.

He shuddered. Did they shoot patients in this place?

When he looked back at his captive, he saw the man was staring at him with narrowed eyes, probably fixing his features in his mind so he could give a description later.

Turning away, Gage snatched up the bucket and mop, hoping the props would make him look like part of the janitorial staff.

As soon as the door closed, Tucker started thumping his legs. Gage was tempted to go back and tie him down, but he couldn't spare the time.

Avoiding the wet floor, he strode purposefully toward the stairwell. When he reached the fire door, he hesitated. He'd intended to spring Vanderhoven, but now he realized that staying around this place was too dangerous. If he didn't get off the property quickly, he might not get out at all.

Once he got out, he was going to have a chat with Evan Buckley. If the guy knew what had happened at the lab, Gage was going to get the information out of him.

He sprinted down several flights of steps, praying that he wouldn't run into Riddell or Dumont coming back up, and finally reached the first floor, where he found himself in another hallway.

When a woman stepped from one room into

another, he set his bucket on the floor and started mopping, keeping his head down and his shoulders slumped as though he was tired of washing floors for a living.

As he'd hoped, she didn't give him a second glance as she went about her business. He was one of the invisible legions who took care of the grunt work. She wasn't dressed like a nurse. He guessed this must be the administrative level of the hospital.

So far, it appeared that nobody had cottoned to the unfortunate incident upstairs between the maintenance man and the escaped nut case.

Picking up his bucket and carrying his mop, he turned in the other direction, heading toward the back of the building, wondering if he could get out a window. No such luck. They were all barred.

He felt the hair on the back of his neck prickle when he heard a familiar voice coming from one of the offices.

Dr. Morton.

Gage was tempted to run in the other direction. Instead he walked quietly toward the doorway and stood just out of sight where he could eavesdrop on the conversation. The doctor was talking to someone, then he'd pause and wait for a response. But Gage couldn't hear anyone answering, which meant the doctor must be on the phone.

Pressing himself against the wall, Gage crept closer.

"That's your problem," the doctor said matter-of-factly. He listened for a minute. His voice turned angry when he said, "Don't tell me how to do my job. Of course I understand why we need to keep them isolated."

After a pause, he continued. "You certainly made the right decision having them transferred here. Initially they were quite agitated. They're much calmer now."

Were they talking about him and Vanderhoven? They could be. Of course, there would be a lot of patients here who were agitated when they arrived at the nut house.

After a moment's silence the doctor continued in a more moderate voice. "It would help to know the aftereffects of the lab accident."

Lab accident? That certainly changed the focus of the conversation. Gage waited for some clue about the aftereffects, but Morton only said, "He'll be ready for an interview in a few hours."

Gage wished like hell that he could hear the other end of the exchange. Were they really discussing him? Or could it be Vanderhoven?

Gage fought a wave of nausea as he remembered trying to crawl to safety then passing out.

He needed to find out what they'd been up to in that lab. But Morton was doing a lot more listening than talking. The doctor's voice turned testy when he said, "We're very aware of security precautions here. I don't appreciate your stationing a guard at our facility. And don't tell me that's not the man's regular job. It's his assignment here."

It sounded like they meant Hank Riddell—a reminder that Gage was pressing his luck by hanging around. Turning quickly, he hunched his shoulders again and ambled toward the back of the building.

He came to a door at the end of a corridor. Instead of a knob, it had one of those metal bars that spanned the width at waist height.

When he pushed it, the door swung open. In the next second, an alarm bell began to clang.

With a curse, Gage bolted through the doorway and into the late-afternoon sunshine. As he ran, he realized he was seeing the same view as the one from his room: a wide stretch of green lawn with trees on the far side. If he could reach them, he'd have a chance.

Still weak from his enforced bed rest, he'd made it only a quarter of the way across the lawn before he was gasping for air and fighting a stitch in his side. But he kept running.

When he was about ten yards from the trees, a voice rang out behind him.

"Stop."

Gage speeded up, the breath wheezing in and out of his lungs.

"Stop or I'll shoot."

Gage knew his only option was to plow ahead.

He kept running as fast as he could, the pain in his side almost too much to bear.

Before he reached the woods, he heard a bullet whiz past his head.

Another shot rang out. With a silent thanks to the supreme deity, Gage reached the trees and leaped into the cover that the branches provided, then angled off to the right. In thirty yards, he almost ran into a ten-foot-tall fence made of black vertical rods held together with horizontal cross pieces at the bottom and top. Under ordinary circumstances, he could have scaled it easily. In his present condition, he knew he didn't have a chance.

He kept bearing to his right, but he picked up the sound of someone crunching through the leaves, looking for the escaped prisoner. The guy with the gun. And he seemed to be catching up. No surprise, since he was undoubtedly in better shape than a patient who'd been in bed for days.

Gage had taken out the maintenance man, but he

didn't give much for his chances against an armed opponent. What were they going to do—shoot him and tell the authorities it was self-defense?

Every breath Gage took now was agony, and he knew he couldn't run much farther. When he spotted a fallen log, he stopped short, then dropped down beside it. Digging into the leaves that covered the forest floor, he wedged his body along the lower edge of the fallen trunk and under some branches, praying that up against the log and wearing a gray uniform, he'd be hard to spot.

Footsteps crunched toward him, and he went rigid, holding his breath. When the pursuer sped past, he dragged in air, then lay there panting. He was safe for the moment, but he knew that when the guy didn't catch up soon, he'd double back. And the next time he wouldn't speed on by; he'd be looking for Gage's hiding place.

Gage gave himself a few moments to rest. Then he heaved himself up and started in the other direction, angling toward the fence.

When he reached it, he stopped. Unless he could get past the barrier, he was trapped on the hospital grounds. In frustration, he shook the metal bars, hoping they might have rusted at the top or bottom. No such luck.

But as he held on to the vertical rods, wishing

they'd open up for him, something truly strange happened. The solid metal seemed to give a little, and when he dragged his hands apart, the upright shafts bent as though they were made of hard rubber.

Elated, he pulled again and felt the bars bend, opening a space in the fence. When it was just wide enough to accommodate his body, he slipped through. Then he took an extra moment to pull the barrier back into place so nobody would know how and where he'd gotten out.

Before Riddell or whoever it was could come back and spot him, he took off through the woods, running as fast as he could, which was about as fast as a wounded water buffalo.

He almost blundered into a creek. Stopping before he got his pant legs wet, he found some stepping stones and crossed, working hard to keep his balance. He needed to rest. But he was afraid to stop so close to the hospital grounds.

On the other side of the creek, he spotted several houses. When he saw shapes waving in the breeze, he froze, till he realized he was seeing laundry flapping on a line in back of a clapboard rancher.

Grateful for the gathering dusk, he slipped from tree to tree, studying the back of the house. He could see a woman in the kitchen, preparing a meal, but she was looking down.

Taking a chance that her husband wasn't lurking around with a shotgun, he hurried to the clothesline and took down a pair of jeans and a dark T-shirt.

With his booty tucked under his arm, he ran along through the woods for fifty more yards, then shucked his janitor's clothes and pulled on the new ones. He balled up the uniform and shoved it into a pile of leaves someone had raked into the woods.

Then he allowed himself ten minutes rest sitting against a tree trunk with his head thrown back. He wanted to fall over and go to sleep. Instead he walked back to the road and ambled along more slowly, like a guy out for a stroll.

He had a lot to think about—starting with the assumption that he'd been exposed to a dangerous chemical agent in that lab accident.

It hadn't killed him. But he was pretty sure it had done *something*. And he wanted to wrap his mind around exactly what that was.

He'd had some lucky breaks in the past hour. But were they really luck?

He'd badly wanted to get out of the restraints holding his wrists, and they'd loosened. He'd thought the door to his room was locked, then it had opened for him when he'd grasped the knob.

And finally there was the totally strange business with the fence. It was made of solid metal bars designed to keep the nut cases inside the hospital grounds. Yet when he'd pulled on them, they'd opened up for him as though he'd been parting thin tree branches.

So where was he going with that information? He might be an impulsive guy, but when he stopped to study a dangerous or questionable situation, he tried to use logic. In this case, logic told him he was thinking something that had to be impossible. At the same time, logic also told him that the recent experiences added up to a pretty strange conclusion.

Stopping, he looked around and spotted a length of fence post that might have fallen from the back of someone's pickup truck. Gingerly, he retrieved it from the ground, hefting it in his hands. It was about four inches in diameter, strong and solid, and he thought that what he was planning to try with it was crazy.

Still, he carried it into the woods and went ahead with the plan, holding the wood out in front of him, balancing it on his flattened hands and focusing on the physical act of breaking it across the middle.

For several seconds, he thought that he'd let his imagination run away with him. But he kept pouring mental energy into the experiment, picturing what he wanted to happen and keeping his hands flat so that he wasn't exerting any physical pressure on the post.

He felt a kind of vibration go through the wood. Then he heard a crack as the fence post broke into two pieces, falling to the ground near his feet.

He'd come up with the experiment as a test of his theory. Still, he stared at the wood in astonishment, trying to wrap his head around what had just happened.

He hadn't broken the fence post with physical strength. Even under the best of circumstances, he couldn't snap a four-inch-diameter pole using brute force. He'd done it with his mind.

Impossible. Yet the broken post lay on the ground at his feet. Unless he was under the influence of some delusion.

Confusion. Delusion. Maybe that was the side effect of the drug he'd been exposed to.

Another thought struck him, and he went stock-still. Suppose that was the main purpose? He knew that Cranesbrook had some Defense Department contracts. What if the lab had sold the department on the idea of dousing enemy troops with happy gas? Like those insane CIA LSD experiments in the sixties.

Squatting down, he picked up one of the halves

of the fence post and hurled it into the woods. It sailed through the air and landed with a satisfying thunk that made a squirrel scramble up a tree.

Maybe he and the squirrel were on the same drug trip. Or maybe the chemical had effects nobody knew about.

Because strange as it seemed, as far as he could tell, he'd broken the piece of wood with his mind. And not just the wood. He'd gotten out of the restraints, opened the door to his room and bent iron posts.

He had a new ability he hadn't been born with. Which led to another conclusion. Suppose the chemical was designed to give *our* troops special abilities? Or what if someone had been tampering with the Cranesbrook experiments?

Like maybe Evan Buckley. Had somebody paid him to screw up the procedure in Lab 7? Was that why he'd been acting weird for the past few weeks? Were he and Riddell working together?

Or had it been Bray? The thought flicked through Gage's brain cells, and he tried to shove it away. But he couldn't totally dismiss it. Bray had been behaving strangely too. He'd needed money—badly—to pay for his sister's hospital bills. What would he have been willing to do to build up his bank account before he disappeared?

The "why" would have to wait until later. Gage didn't know what to believe or who was behind the lab accident. He only knew the consequences. He'd like to compare notes with Vanderhoven.

Still, he had come to another important conclusion. Whoever had released that chemical agent didn't know what the effect had been on him. If they had, they would have known it was useless to hold him with cuffs and locked doors.

He felt a burst of adrenaline shoot through his body and had to stop himself from shouting out loud. Super powers! He'd turned into a secret super hero.

Well, not quite, he cautioned himself. He could work some neat tricks with his mind, but he wasn't going to take a chance on trying to stop a speeding bullet. He could, however, think of a lot of exciting possibilities for his new talent.

Down the road, he heard a car coming toward him and tensed. But it drove on by. Still, the intrusion served as a reminder. He was an escaped mental patient. Obviously dangerous—judging by what he'd just done.

How much power did he have? Could he perfect the talent? And would it stay with him? That was an interesting consideration. What if this new skill was only temporary and it crapped out on him just when he needed it? Or what if there was a limit to how much he could do in a given period of time?

He didn't know how long he'd be able to work magic with his mind, or how reliable the skill would be, but he'd enjoy it while it lasted.

He kept walking north until he came to a house where several newspapers lay scattered in the driveway.

Looking toward the front window, he saw a light burning, but he'd bet it was a decoy. Still he approached the structure with caution.

In the Special Forces, he'd learned how to hotwire an old car. Maybe now he could do better.

After waiting several minutes, he walked around the back of the house and found a two-year-old Chevrolet parked by the kitchen entrance.

The car doors were locked. But when he held the handle and thought about working the mechanism, the lock clicked open. Sliding into the driver's seat, he thought about turning the ignition. That was a little more complicated. But several seconds later, the car roared to life. Hot damn!

If he wanted to lead a life of crime, this new twist sure came in handy. He didn't have any money. Maybe he should stop and borrow some from an ATM. He'd keep track of what he took and pay it back later.

If he were a criminal, the prospect of free access to ATMs would be pretty exciting. But he wasn't. He'd been a law-abiding citizen all his life. He'd served in the military with distinction. And he'd started a security company with his friend Brayden Sloane when they'd gotten out of the service three years ago.

Now he'd sunk to the status of escaped nut case.

He felt his chest tighten. The first thing he needed to do was go home and tell Lily he was okay.

A pang of conscience grabbed him. He'd tried to be a good husband, but he knew he'd been neglecting his wife. Now the reasons didn't even seem important.

After Five Star had gotten the Cranesbrook contract, Bray had taken the brunt of the new work. Then Bray's sister had needed his help with her hospital bills and with her new baby, and Gage had stepped in to pull up the slack. He'd started spending more and more time on the Eastern Shore. That was a mistake. He should have figured out how to stay in the Baltimore office and spend more hours at home. He and Lily should be a team. They should sit down and talk about their goals, their hopes for the future.

One thing captivity had made clear: Now that he was in trouble, he needed to know Lily was on his side. He thought about calling her. But he couldn't explain everything that had happened over the phone. And he needed to feel her arms around him. Needed the pressure of her lips on his. If he could hold her, kiss her, he'd figure out the rest.

But first he had to get home.

He was pretty sure the cops were looking for him by now, so maybe he'd better leave this car down by the docks in St. Stephens and not drive across the Bay Bridge. Instead, he'd go by water.

Boats were different from cars. Unless the owner was an oyster man or a crabber or something like that, he left his boat in the marina during the week and only went out on some weekends. He could borrow a pleasure craft, and nobody would miss it. If he motored up the Miles River and then across the bay, he'd be home faster than if he drove.

St. Stephens was a tourist town, with art galleries, craft boutiques, real estate offices and T-shirt shops lining Main Street. For the convenience of visitors, large parking lots filled an open area near the harbor.

After leaving the stolen car in one of the lots, Gage strolled toward the dock. Stopping at a metal container that sold newspapers, he looked at the date on the front page of the *Baltimore Sun*. It was five days after the accident.

He'd suspected he'd been out of commission for a while. Still, the news was a shock, and he leaned against a railing, sucking in air. No wonder he was so wobbly. He'd been in bed most of a week.

When he was feeling better, he strolled onto the dock as though he belonged there, covertly inspecting the boats for something that would suit his purposes. He wanted fast transportation, and a craft that was small enough for him to handle by himself. He also wanted to be able to get out of the wind if the weather turned nasty.

When he came to a small cabin cruiser called *Four Play*, he did a double take. What a jerk of a name. He supposed four guys had bought it together. Did they take turns bringing party girls down here on weekends?

Too bad someone was going to be disappointed Saturday morning, because their little beauty was perfect for his purposes. But he'd leave it where the cops could find it when he got to Baltimore.

PATROLMAN MAXINE WALLACE took off her cap and ran a hand through her red curls, glad that the sun had finally set.

Replacing her cap, she trained her blue eyes on the driveway leading toward the Beech Grove Clinic.

When a late-model Ford pulled toward her, she straightened.

She'd responded to an emergency call from the clinic. But as a small-town cop, she wasn't equipped to handle a heavy-duty investigation, so she'd alerted the State Police, as per her standing orders.

The car doors opened, and two tall, capable-looking men got out. One had dark hair; the other was a blonde. At eight in the evening, they were wearing business suits and wrinkled shirts. It looked like they'd put in a full day, having gotten the call just before they were about to knock off.

"Maxine Wallace?"

"Yes."

"Randall McClellan," the dark-haired one said.

"And Richard Francis. Maryland State Police."

They shook hands. She didn't resent calling in the big guns; her small department simply didn't have the investigative or lab resources of the state cops.

"What have we got here?" McClellan asked.

"An escaped patient and a murdered maintenance man."

"The patient is the chief suspect?"

"Yes. A man named Gage Darnell. Apparently he was in some kind of accident at the Cranesbrook Lab and went berserk. They were trying to stabilize him when he escaped."

"He was violent?"

"Yes. They said he was in restraints."

"Then how did he get away?"

"Good question. They don't know."

"Who's the vic?"

"A janitor named Tucker Hillman. Let me show you the supposed murder scene."

"Supposed?" Francis asked.

"Something's fishy," she answered as she led them around the building. "It looks to me like it's been disturbed, at the very least."

"Oh, yeah?" the other detective asked.

"The victim is in a toolshed on the grounds. But I think he was murdered somewhere else and dumped there."

"Why?"

She shrugged. "It just looks wrong to me. I think there are drag marks outside."

"Okay."

"Also, he died of blunt instrument trauma, and head wounds bleed. But there's no blood on the ground," she said over her shoulder as she opened the door of the shed.

She'd already cordoned off the area with yellow crime scene tape. The dead man lay sprawled on the cement floor, face down, a bloody dent in the back of his head.

The two detectives made a quick inspection. Then McClellan pulled out his phone. "We need a CSI team at the Beech Grove Clinic. And a meat wagon."

Maxie knew the body would be taken to the morgue in Baltimore where all autopsies in the state were handled.

Snapping the phone closed, the detective turned to her. "I don't want anyone else messing around with the scene. You stay here and keep the curious away until the lab techs get here. We'll start questioning the staff."

Maxie nodded. She would have liked to be in on the questioning, but she understood the way the system worked. Uniformed cops got the guard duty. Detectives got to ask the questions.

LILY WAS halfway through the dinner shift, taking a break from the heat and noise and frantic activity of the kitchen. She'd been at her work station since before lunch, but she hadn't had anything to eat herself. Now she was thinking she'd better grab something or she was going to fall flat on her face into a frying pan.

But could she choke down anything?

She was still trying to decide what to do when her

cell phone rang. On edge, she snatched the instrument from her pocket and pressed the Talk button.

"Hello."

"Mrs. Darnell?

"Yes."

"I'm glad I reached you."

"Who is this?"

"Dr. Morton from the Beech Grove Clinic."

She dragged in a breath, then let it out in a rush. The man had avoided her since the accident. Now he was contacting her? Apparently, something had happened. Maybe he was calling to say that Gage was on his way home.

Her mouth had turned dry, but she managed to ask, "Yes?"

"I'm afraid we have some bad news."

Her hand clenched around the receiver. Oh Lord, was he going to tell her Gage was dead?

Barely able to breathe, she waited for the doctor's next words. When they came, her brain could hardly interpret what she was hearing.

"Your husband killed a maintenance worker and broke out of the hospital."

"What?"

He repeated the terrible news.

"No!" Her knees buckled, and she dropped into a chair.

"Mrs. Darnell."

"Yes," she answered, her voice sounding as though it was coming from a long way off.

"If he tries to contact you, you need to inform the police. He's a danger to himself and to others if he's at large."

"I don't believe it.

"I'm afraid it's true."

"How?" she managed.

"Mr. Darnell escaped from his room and attacked the man. The back of his head was bashed in."

The vivid picture that leaped into her mind made her suck in a strangled breath. Was that why he was giving her the gory details—so she'd believe him?

"The Maryland State police are on the way to your house."

"Oh," was all she could manage.

"Mr. Darnell is in the grip of paranoid delusions. It's not safe for you to be in your house, in case your husband is heading for home."

"I…I have to get some things," she mumbled, thinking that she could go to Pam's.

And quit in the middle of the dinner shift?

Well, if she got fired that was the least of her worries.

Chapter Four

Gage was feeling better by the time he reached Baltimore's Inner Harbor. He'd enjoyed steering the sweet little craft across the bay. Maybe the guys who'd bought *Four Play* were jerks, but they sure knew how to pick a boat. And piloting their baby had helped him decompress.

Now he was ready to explain to his wife where he'd been for the past few days and ask her to help him hide out.

He backtracked that thought a couple of notches. He'd try to explain as much as he knew. He still hadn't figured out why Dr. Morton had been holding him captive, but he had come to one interesting conclusion. Morton had been talking about a lab accident. So did he think some experiment had gone wrong, as opposed to an explosive device planted in the closet?

He docked *Four Play* in a conveniently vacant

slip, secured the line and strolled up the dock whistling a nautical tune.

Adjacent to the dock was a long-term parking lot for boat owners where he borrowed a car, using the same method he'd employed outside St. Stephens.

He'd get home, tell Lily he'd busted out of the loony bin and apologize for being such a jerk lately. When he'd gotten that out of the way, they could decide on his next step.

What time was it, anyway? Would she be home from work? He glanced at the clock on the dashboard. It was just nine. She wouldn't be there yet, but he could get showered while he was waiting.

The radio was tuned to a classical station playing some kind of jangly modern piece that set his nerves on edge.

He started twisting the knob, looking for an oldies station when an announcer's urgent voice stopped him.

"...Special news bulletin. A dangerous mental patient has escaped from a facility on the Eastern Shore and may be on the way to the Baltimore area."

Gage's breath froze in his lungs. He almost plowed through a red light, then managed to stop in the middle of the crosswalk.

A pedestrian glared at him, but he kept his eyes straight ahead as he listened to the bulletin.

"Gage Darnell, a former security guard at Cranesbrook Associates, escaped from the Beech Grove Clinic this afternoon. Darnell is suspected of attacking and killing a maintenance worker in a toolshed on the grounds of the private sanatorium, before fleeing the facility. He is five feet eleven inches tall. One hundred and seventy pounds. Dark hair worn short in a military cut. Dark brown eyes. Early thirties. He is dangerous. Do not approach him. Call the police if you see him."

Incredulous, Gage stared at the radio receiver, hoping he'd heard that wrong. When a horn sounded behind him, he glanced at the light and saw it had turned green. Jerking his foot onto the accelerator, he lurched across the intersection.

An angry driver sped around him, shouting an obscenity. But he had bigger problems than someone's road rage.

Murder.

His curse rang out inside the empty car. The last time he'd seen Tucker, the guy had been glaring at him and struggling to get free of his bonds. So what the hell had happened between then and now?

Gage drove for a few blocks on automatic pilot, trying to make sense of the news report. He'd left the guy alive! At least that's how he remembered it. The man hadn't been seriously hurt, had he?

Suddenly, he couldn't be sure of his own memory. Maybe he *had* killed the janitor.

Maybe this was like that book by Stephen King. What was it called? *The Dead Zone.* A guy had been in an accident, then a coma for almost five years. When he'd woken up, he'd had special powers. But he'd also had something bad, too. A brain tumor that was going to kill him.

Gage had awakened with special powers. Had he also gotten a dose of something bad? Like, for example, were his memories all scrambled up?

He didn't think so. But then he didn't think he was crazy either. Maybe Dr. Morton was right. Maybe he was dangerous.

As he struggled with his own doubts, his stomach clenched into a painful knot.

"Calm down," he told himself. "You're a logical guy. Tucker is dead. And…and you left him alive and kicking in a closet, not a shed on the grounds."

He clung to that small but important detail like a shipwreck survivor clinging to wooden plank floating in the ocean.

He had to believe in himself, otherwise he was nowhere. He knew he was in trouble, but he'd get himself out of it. He couldn't trust anyone else to do it. His plans had changed abruptly, though. He couldn't hook up with Lily, because the last thing he wanted to do was drag her into his mess.

He pressed down on the accelerator, knowing that he needed to go home and get some clothing and equipment. And he had to get there fast—before Lily got home.

As he drove, his mind sifted through the facts and tried to come up with a scenario that made sense.

Someone else had killed Tucker. Morton? Nurse Ratched? Someone else on the staff? Riddell?

He didn't know who it was. And he didn't know why Tucker had been offed. To shut him up? To give the cops a reason for going after an escaped criminal?

He couldn't figure out the motivation, but whatever had gone down, the Maryland State Police had Gage Darnell pegged as a murder suspect. That was going to make it a hell of a lot harder to find out what had happened at the Beech Grove Clinic. He wasn't just a mental patient on the run. Now he was a murder suspect.

As he turned onto his street, the clock on the dashboard told him it was nine-thirty. He still had time to get in and out before Lily came home from work.

He could grab some clothes and equipment he needed, then get out of there before she heard the escaped-mental-patient report.

He intended to zip up his driveway till he decided it would make more sense if nobody knew he was home. So instead he kept going to the property next door. The elderly Winslows had owned the house until, after her husband died, Mrs. Winslow had sold out to a younger couple.

The neighbors had been appalled when the new owners had torn down the structure with the intention of putting up a McMansion that was bigger than anything else on the street. So far new construction hadn't started, so the lot sat empty. And presented a hazard in the dark, Gage decided as he climbed out of his stolen car, then waited for his eyes to adjust to the low light conditions.

Cautiously, he started forward, then stopped short to avoid tumbling into the gaping hole that had been the basement. Cursing silently, he picked his way around the obstacle course. When he finally made it onto his own property, he went directly to the detached garage, where he started throwing equipment into a couple of cardboard boxes.

He hated to waste the time, going back and forth through the woods, but he figured it was better not to make two trips at the end of his visit. So he carried the boxes back to his stolen car, then dashed to the back door of the house, where they'd hidden a key under a fake rock near the stoop.

After disconnecting the alarm system, he stopped short, fighting a wrenching feeling as he looked around the living room. It was all so familiar. So normal. His leather chair sat in the corner facing the large-screen television. The stained-glass lamp Lily had inherited from her grandmother was on the marble-topped chest under the window.

And his throat clogged when he saw that she'd left her apron draped over the back of a kitchen chair.

He crossed the room and opened the refrigerator where he found a pot of chili. So she *had* made one of his favorites.

She must have fixed it for the weekend, when she'd thought he was coming home. It was full. She hadn't eaten any.

He couldn't stop himself from spooning some into a small bowl, then putting the bowl in the microwave.

He ate a spoonful, savoring the taste. Closing his eyes, he tried to imagine what would have happened if he'd left the security detail to one of his hired hands and come home.

His whole life would be different now. He would have eaten dinner with Lily. No, he would have made love with Lily then enjoyed a leisurely dinner, probably on trays in bed.

He grinned as he imagined the two of them upstairs warm and intimate like in the old days.

The old days?

That would be nine months ago, before he'd started putting in so many hours at Cranesbrook. He'd thought it was worth it because he and Bray were establishing a reputation with Five Star.

Yeah, right. He'd acquired a reputation as a mental patient and murderer. And Bray was missing. Where the hell was he? Hiding out, letting Gage take the heat? Or had they carted him off to some other mental hospital? Or was he dead? The hairs on the back of Gage's neck prickled. Yeah, Bray could be dead, and somebody was covering it up.

Gage clenched his hands in frustration. He was just guessing about Bray. But he knew his own life would never be normal again until he found out what had really happened at the Cranesbrook lab and cleared himself of the murder charge. And even when he did, the taint of scandal would always hang over him. Who was going to hire a security expert who had been a murder suspect? They'd remember the charge, not the acquittal.

He indulged in another curse. When he realized he was still holding the bowl of chili, he set it down on the counter with a clunk and ran upstairs to get some clothes, some money and a weapon.

He thought about writing Lily a note. Maybe he'd be able to do that, if he had the time.

He was just crossing the kitchen with a duffel bag when the back door opened and his wife stepped in.

He wanted to rush to her, fold her close and hang on tight the way he'd dreamed of doing. But the look on her face stopped him in his tracks.

He shifted his weight from one foot to the other, thinking that he never would have imagined this scene in a million years. "I guess you're not welcoming me with open arms."

When she answered with a small nod, he added, "For your information, I didn't do it."

"Didn't do what?" she answered carefully.

"Murder that maintenance man."

He watched her features tighten. "If you didn't do it, how do you know about it?"

"I heard it on the radio on the way over here."

Her barely perceptible nod made his insides twist.

"I left the guy locked in a closet. The news report says they found his body in a shed on the grounds." When she didn't speak, he went on. "He was in the hall, mopping the floor when I broke out of my room. I tied him up and gagged him and left him where he'd be found. I didn't carry him outside to the shed. After five days in bed on heavy sedation, I didn't have the strength to carry anyone. And I didn't kill him. Somebody else did that."

The long speech left him feeling like a kid trying to explain how come his softball was sitting on the living-room floor, though he wasn't the one who had broken the window. Too bad this was a lot more serious than some broken glass.

When she said nothing, he kept talking, because that was his only option. "It's a setup. They framed me."

Her throat worked. "Who? Why?"

He made a frustrated gesture. "To cover something up? To get the cops to shoot first and ask questions later?"

It was obvious she didn't know whether to believe him.

"Cover up what?" she whispered.

He held out his hands, palm up. "I think it goes back to the explosion in Lab 7. It's supposed to be an accident. Maybe it was really sabotage. I'm not sure, but I need to find out."

The stark lines of her face softened. Just a little. He felt as if he was making progress. If he could hold her in his arms, connect with her physically and help her remember what they meant to each other, he thought he could get her on his side.

With the luxury of time, he might have won her over. Before either of them got a chance to speak again, a loud knock sounded on the front door.

Her gaze shot to the front of the house, then back to him.

"Ask who it is," he ordered.

She took a step toward the front hall. "Who is it?" she called out in a quavery voice.

"Police."

"Perfect," he muttered. Watching her fixed gaze and her rigid shoulders, he thought she was calculating her chances of making a run for it.

"You'd better get out of here," she said, her voice high and thin.

"It's not that easy. They'll have the front and back doors covered. Tell them you need a minute."

She heaved in a breath and let it out in a rush. "Just a minute," she called out.

With time running out, Gage made a life-and-death decision. "You're coming with me."

Her eyes widened in alarm. "No."

"I can't let them capture me. I need you to get me out of the house."

"If you're innocent…"

"Screw innocent," he spat out. "I told you, somebody framed me."

When he pulled out the gun he'd jammed into the waistband of his slacks, she gasped. "Gage?"

"I'm sorry. You can get me out of here. They won't shoot at you," he said, praying that it was true. "If there are two of them, they've probably got both doors blocked by now. I parked over at the Winslows'. Pick up my duffel bag and hold it in your arms."

When she just stood there, he barked, "Hurry up."

The fear on her face made him physically sick, but he couldn't see any alternative. She didn't have enough information to trust him. And he couldn't allow himself to be caught—not when he knew somebody had pinned a murder charge on him. He had no choice, he told himself.

He thrust the duffel toward her, and she wrapped it in her arms. Taking her elbow, he pointed her toward the front door. "Don't try anything tricky, or you're likely to get us both killed," he said as he ushered her down the hall.

When they reached the door, he paused. The porch lamp was on. Through the side light, he could see a tall man dressed in a suit standing on the other side of the door. But the light in the front hall was turned off, so he knew the guy couldn't see inside.

"This is Gage Darnell. I've taken Lily Darnell hostage. I'm leaving by the front door. I have a gun at her back. If you make any wrong moves, she's likely to get hurt. Throw your weapons down and back off."

"Darnell, we just want to talk to you."

"Don't give me that crap. You think I murdered someone. And it's not going to do me any good to tell you I didn't do it. So throw down your weapons."

"You're only making things worse, Darnell."

Gage wasn't going to argue about that. Not when the guy might be signaling his partner to call for backup. "Drop your weapon and back off before Lily gets hurt."

For a long moment, Gage was afraid the detective was going to do something stupid. But he finally complied.

When the gun was on the porch floor, Gage opened the front door, and kicked the weapon into a flower bed, keeping his eyes on the detective. The man was tall, dark-haired and about his own age. Under better circumstances, they would have been on the same side.

They eyed each other.

"Raise your hands in the air and back up," he ordered. The man glanced at Lily, then did as Gage asked.

He kept his voice calm and low, even while his heart was pounding inside his chest. "Down the stairs and into the yard. Call out to your partner and tell him not to shoot. Neither one of us wants to see my wife stuck in the middle of a firefight."

The man glared at him, then shouted, "Richard, come around front and don't shoot. Darnell is taking his wife out at gunpoint."

Knowing the situation was still far too dangerous, Gage watched the other detective step around the side of the house. He was holding a handgun. "Get rid of your weapon. Then raise your hands. Come into the light where I can see you," Gage ordered, moving forward so that Lily had to walk down the front steps. He could feel her trembling, and he prayed she could get through this without doing something they'd both regret.

When they were all standing in the yard, he said. "I know everyone claims innocence, but in this case it's true. Somebody framed me. That guy was alive when I left him in a utility closet. On the third floor. The left side of the building as you face the back. We never got near any toolshed."

"So you say."

"How was he killed?"

The detective looked like he was considering

his options. Finally he said, "Blunt instrument to the back of the head."

"I didn't have any weapons with me. I left him tied up down the hall from the room where they had me in restraints. See what you find up there. And look for a couple of bullets embedded in one of the trees out back. Somebody shot at me when I crossed the lawn."

"Uh-huh."

"Don't judge me until you collect some evidence."

"We've got the evidence of kidnapping right now," the blond one said. "Unless you turn your hostage loose."

"Not until I'm out of here."

Neither cop's expression changed. Gage knew that pulling this stunt was stacking the case against himself, but he simply couldn't take a chance on letting them take him in.

He saw their unmarked car in the driveway in back of Lily's. Stopping beside it, he leaned against the fender, keeping his gaze on the enemy but sending his mind into the engine's inner workings. Lucky he had some mechanic's skills. Without letting go of Lily, he used his new talent to fuse some wires in the electrical system so there was no chance of the car starting.

"Stay where you are," he warned. "If you follow me into the woods, she's going to get hurt."

"You're not acting like an innocent guy," the dark-haired detective observed.

"Unfortunately, that's true," he agreed, "But that's the way it goes. If you know what's good for Lily, give us five minutes head start."

He backed away, still holding his wife, facing the cops.

When they reached the trees that separated his house from the ruined property next door, she finally spoke.

"Please, let me go."

"I can't. Not yet."

As soon as the cops were out of sight, he tucked the gun back into his waistband, then took the duffel bag from her. Grabbing her left arm, he dragged her along as he hustled her toward the stolen car.

She stumbled over some debris strewn on the ground, and he held her up, steering her around the open foundation to the car that he was glad he'd positioned for a fast getaway.

He tossed the duffel bag into the back before helping her into the driver's seat.

Pulling the gun out again, he ran around to the other side and climbed in, seeing that she was fumbling for the key, probably hoping she could get away. But the key wasn't there.

When he used his mind to start the engine, she gave a little cry.

"Drive," he said, pointing the gun at her.

"How did you do that?"

"My electronics equipment," he said, because he didn't think she was going to believe the real explanation. "Drive us out of here," he added.

"Where?"

"When you get to the street, turn right." He'd been thinking about where he could go, and he'd remembered a place where he might be safe for a while.

As soon as Darnell disappeared, Rand McClellan scrambled for the flower bed and retrieved his gun. His partner did the same.

Armed again, they dashed into the woods, thinking they were heading for the house next door.

Rand sped up, pounding through the woods. In the darkness, he made out an open area, and he thought it might provide a shortcut.

"This way."

They both dashed toward the wide gap in the trees. Suddenly, the ground fell away. Rand gasped as his next step landed on empty air. He was tumbling into space when Richard grabbed the back of his coat and pulled him to safety.

They both fell backward onto a pile of dirt, panting.

"What the hell was that?" Richard said as he stood up and brushed off his suit pants.

Rand stood and took a cautious step forward. "It looks like somebody knocked down the house and left the basement," he observed dryly. "Lucky I didn't land on the cement floor."

The conversation came to a halt when they heard a car start. "The bastard's getting away."

By mutual agreement, they turned and dashed back the way they'd come, avoiding the hole. As they reached their vehicle, Rand jumped into the driver's seat. Richard took his place on the passenger side.

But when Rand cranked the ignition, nothing happened. He tried again. Nada. Not even a screeching sound.

"Now what?"

Rand popped the hood and got out. Richard reached for the flashlight in the glove compartment and joined him at the front of the car, where Richard played the light over the engine.

They'd worked together long enough to develop a rhythm. Neither one of them was out to make a point. They were both willing to lean on their own strengths and let their partner fill in the missing pieces.

Since Rand knew almost nothing about cars, he looked expectantly at his partner. "Find anything?"

Richard stared into the bowels of the engine, pointing with the flashlight beam. "See there? Some of the electrical wires are fused."

"How?"

"Hell if I know. The car was fine when we drove in here."

Rand cleared his throat. "You saw Darnell stop beside the front end. Do you think he put a voodoo hex on it?"

"I don't believe in voodoo hexes," Richard snapped.

"Unfortunately, neither do I. Maybe it overheated. Or maybe he had some kind of special electronics equipment. I heard that was his thing."

Richard nodded. "But the main point is, we've lost Darnell, and we're going to have to hitch a ride." He pulled out his cell phone and called in to headquarters.

Then they took the flashlight back to the property next door on the off chance that Darnell had left his wife in the woods before he split. When they called her name, however, nobody answered. Now that they had a light, they could see the gaping hole in the ground.

Rand whistled. "I could have broken my neck falling in there. Thanks for the quick save, partner."

Richard made a grunting sound. He'd never been the type to take praise easily.

They walked around the crater to the driveway, which was still more or less intact.

"Mrs. Darnell?" Rand called.

Still no answer.

"I guess he took her for insurance," Richard said.

"Do you think he's going to hurt her?"

"Don't know, but she looked scared. I wouldn't want to be in her shoes. On the run with an escaped mental patient."

"We don't even know what car he's driving."

"Yeah. But where can he go?"

"We'll figure it out."

"TURN RIGHT AGAIN," Gage ordered.

Lily slid him a sidewise glance. His face was set in a grim line. He looked tense and frustrated. Had he really gone off the deep end? Would he hurt her?

She knew Gage could be impulsive. Some might call him a hothead. But never in a million years did she think he'd be accused of murder then kidnap her in order to get away.

She might have been able to stop him. Like, what if she'd dropped to the porch floor when he'd hustled her out of the house? She didn't think he would have shot her. But she couldn't even be sure of that.

She turned her head toward him, staring at the rigid line of his jaw. "Let me go," she said in a low voice.

"No."

"Why not?"

"I want to convince you that I haven't done anything wrong."

"You've already missed your chance."

"Turn left at the next light," he said in a gritty voice.

She slowed at the intersection and turned. "Give me a clue where we're going."

The Wilson estate, he thought, but he didn't say it out loud, in case she managed to get away before they reached their destination. He simply couldn't take a chance on that.

"Harford County."

"Okay."

"I'm sorry."

"About what?"

"Scaring you. Dragging you along with me."

"All I have to do is pull over to the curb and get out. Then you can be on your way." She flicked a look at him. "Please, Gage?"

Chapter Five

Gage's answer came from his gut. "No!"

He heard Lily swallow in the darkness. Logic told him that he *should* let her go. That was the honorable thing to do.

He was dragging her into a heap of danger where she didn't belong. But now that she was with him, he couldn't sever the connection.

He wanted to say, "I need you so much. Stick with me. I'll prove to you that I didn't kill anyone. And I'll show you I'm ready to stop messing up our marriage."

Yeah, sure. He'd just taken a giant leap forward in messmaking.

She had to be thinking he'd screwed up royally. He'd proved it by taking her hostage. Plus, he'd been AWOL so much for the past few months, they'd already been as good as separated. And no reason to trust him, either. Still, he clung to the hope that if he kept her close, maybe he had a chance to change the equation.

He knew he couldn't articulate any of that convoluted thinking, so he said, "I woke up in the hospital. They were holding me against my will. Lord knows what they'll do to me now."

"If someone is acting irrationally they can't let him run loose," she said in a flat voice that made his blood run cold.

"I'm not irrational!"

"But you killed someone to get out of there?" she inquired, as though they were talking about his finding a dead mouse in a trap under the sink.

"No!" He struggled to see this situation from her point of view—and struggled to keep the hysteria from his voice. Pretending he was perfectly calm, he asked, "How did you hear about... the murder?"

"Dr. Morton called."

"Nice of him. Did you get him to talk to you before I broke out?"

"No."

"Yeah, well, that's a clue to his level of cooperation, don't you think?"

She answered with a barely perceptible nod.

Pressing his small advantage, he asked, "What else did the good doctor say?"

"Not much. I know you were exposed to a dangerous chemical at Cranesbrook." She sighed. Probably she'd decided she had nothing to lose by talking to him. "I went down there, but nobody would give me any information. Then Amelia St. James called and threatened to fire me if I didn't come back to work."

He made an angry sound. "She's a real gem."

"Tell me about the maintenance man," she whispered.

"After I got out of my room we ran into each other in the hall. He was going to pull the fire alarm, so I punched him on the chin, tied him up and left him in a supply closet. When I closed the door, he was very much alive and glaring at me."

"You should turn yourself in and explain that you didn't kill him before you get into worse trouble."

He barked out a laugh. "Like hell. Somebody framed me, and I'll bet Dr. Morton is in on it."

"He said you'd be paranoid."

"Perfect!" He caught himself again and struggled to sound as though he wasn't losing his marbles. "You'd be paranoid, too, if you woke up strapped into a bed and nobody would tell you what was going on."

She winced. He hoped it was a good sign.

"If you were strapped to a bed, how did you escape?"

"I don't know," he answered, thinking that it wasn't exactly a lie. "Maybe somebody forgot to tighten the restraints. Anyhow, I wiggled out of them."

"Uh-huh." She seemed to be waiting for the real explanation, which he wasn't going to give her. She already thought he was crazy. If he started talking about his new talent, she'd be even more convinced that his brain had snapped. So he skipped that part of the story and went on.

"When I got down to the office level, I heard Morton talking on the phone. I can't be sure who was on the other end, but it was someone connected with Cranesbrook. When the smoke bomb went off in the lab, it dropped me, and now they're trying to cover it up. They even had a guy from Cranesbrook over at the hospital watching me."

"I was at the hospital a few days ago, and Morton said you were alternately violent and out of it. Is that true?" she asked.

"I don't know," he answered honestly.

"Then how do you know you didn't hit that maintenance guy with something?"

"I...I..." He caught his breath and tried again.

"I left him in the building. He was found dead in a toolshed. It doesn't match up."

"Are you sure you're remembering it right?" she pressed, bringing back his own doubts.

"Stop making me question my own sanity," he shouted.

When she took her lower lip between her teeth, he leaned back in his seat and tried to tamp down his tension. He was on edge and worn out, and too recently out of bed for his present level of exertion. He needed to rest as soon as they got to the Wilson estate.

Larry Wilson had hired Five Star Security to install a state-of-the-art security system at the mansion he owned in Harford County, partly because he was going to be out of town for several months. Gage hoped he hadn't changed his plans and that he'd be safe there.

He shook his head. Who was he kidding?

He wasn't safe anywhere.

LILY KEPT her eyes on the road, but she was all too aware of the man sitting next to her. Her husband, Gage. She'd thought she knew him. Now he might as well be a madman who had grabbed her at random off the street.

He'd always radiated an edge of danger. Tonight

the danger was right there, front and center. Tension surrounded him like sparks snapping from the broken end of a downed power line.

They'd been through some bad times together but she never would have predicted *this*.

Or more accurately, she never would have predicted that she'd be afraid of Gage Darnell at a deep, gut-wrenching level. But she was.

Her heart was pounding as she kept driving, waiting for his next direction. Too bad she didn't have her cell phone. But he'd hustled her out of the house without anything besides the clothes on her back.

Which argued for the theory that Gage hadn't come home with the idea of abducting her. He'd just gotten caught by the cops and used her as a convenient shield.

She shuddered. He'd held her at gunpoint, and she still didn't know if he was crazy enough to pull the trigger. He sounded sane, but she'd heard that mental patients could sometimes do that—convince the doctors they were okay so they could get out.

When he turned toward her again, she struggled not to shiver.

"Just let me go," she tried again.

"Can't do that," he shot back.

"Why?"

"I shouldn't have mentioned Harford County. If you tell them about it, maybe they can figure out where I am."

"I don't know where we're going!"

"Good."

She kept driving. Finally, she asked in a low voice, "Do you love me?"

She found herself holding her breath as she waited for his answer.

"Yes."

"Then let me go."

"I want a chance to convince you I'm not a criminal."

She might have pointed out that his method wasn't particularly sound. Instead, she clenched the steering wheel and continued on their one-way trip to hell.

When he directed her onto the beltway, then to Exit 27 and Dulaney Valley Road, she suddenly had a better idea of their destination. While Gage and Bray were working for Cranesbrook, they'd taken a side job installing an alarm system in a mansion up here. Gage had told her that the owners were taking a round-the-world trip, which was why they wanted the property protected.

So the house was empty. Gage knew it and he planned to hide out there.

He confirmed her supposition when he told her to pull up in front of a metal gate blocking a long, private drive.

Taking her with him, he climbed out, then pushed the intercom button. When nobody answered, he punched numbers on the keypad. She wondered how he knew the code, but moments later the gate swung open. After driving through, he closed the barrier, then continued up the driveway to an enormous stone structure that sat brooding in the darkness. As they got close, floodlights switched on, and she could see that the building looked more like a medieval castle than a home.

Gage saw her eyeing the place. "It's got ten bedrooms."

"So I should have some privacy," she murmured, calculating her escape chances. If he'd just leave her alone, she could work out a plan.

In the next moment, he dashed that hope.

"I don't think so," he answered as he drove around the back. "I need to keep an eye on you."

He pulled the car around the side of the house, then let them in through a set of French doors. In response to the beeping from the security system, he hustled Lily to the control panel, where he disabled the alarm.

She watched him press keys once again, but

she didn't bother to ask how he knew the right sequence. She figured he was unlikely to share that information.

RICHARD FRANCIS leaned against the wall across from the utility closet in the wing of the building where Gage Darnell had been confined. He and Rand had been at the end of their shift when they'd caught this case.

Richard had been up for twenty hours, and he needed some sleep. Instead he was back at Beech Grove, watching the crime scene technicians do their thing, and hoping they'd find some evidence that this was the murder scene, not the toolshed.

He wasn't sure why he was rooting for the closet, except that he didn't like Dr. Morton. He suspected that the doctor knew more than he was saying. So what was he hiding?

An hour ago, Richard and his partner had flipped a coin. And he'd won, if you wanted to look at it from that point of view. Rand was stuck with the grunt work—interviewing Five Star employees, searching for clues as to where Darnell might be hiding out.

And Richard was back at the mental hospital checking out the story Darnell had given them, as well as the scenario that Dr. Morton had outlined.

Richard would have liked to search the woods for evidence of the shots that Darnell had talked about. But that was better done by sunlight.

A uniformed cop came running up, looking excited.

"What?" Richard asked.

"We found a hammer at the bottom of the kitchen trash bin. It's got blood on the head."

"Great!" Richard turned to one of the technicians. "We may have found the murder weapon. Run it for fingerprints ASAP."

"You got it."

If it had Darnell's fingerprints, that might prove something. And if it was wiped clean, that might prove something, too. Darnell had been in a hurry to get away. He probably wouldn't have stopped to wipe off the hammer and stuff it in the bottom of a trash bin. But if someone was setting him up, they wouldn't have left their own prints.

GAGE TURNED AWAY from the keypad. Just like at the front gate, he had no idea of the correct security code. But while he'd punched buttons, he'd reached beyond the panel with his mind and disabled the system.

He kept his gaze away from Lily's accusing eyes. It made him sick to know that she was afraid of him, that she thought he'd killed someone. That she thought he might harm *her.*

"When are you going to let me go?" she asked again.

"As soon as I can figure out how to prove I didn't murder anyone."

"Thanks," she whispered, and he guessed she didn't think that would happen anytime soon.

"Come on."

"Where?"

"To check the pantry." He wasn't really hungry, but he knew his body would crash if he didn't keep it fueled.

He took Lily by the arm and steered her down the hall toward the kitchen. She didn't protest, but he watched her gaze darting around. Probably she was looking for escape routes.

They reached the kitchen. Despite the circumstances, he heard her whistle through her teeth as she stared at the gourmet wonderland that boasted two Sub-Zero refrigerators, two professional-quality ranges, miles of granite countertop, and a rack displaying gleaming copper pots.

"This is bigger than the restaurant kitchen. And better-equipped.

"Yeah."

"Somebody here is a gourmet cook."

"Maybe they just want to show how much money they spent on remodeling."

When she lingered near the island, he wondered if she was hoping to find a knife to defend herself. He marched her across to the walk-in pantry, where he found an unopened package of fig cookies.

"Want some?"

She shook her head, but he took the package with him as he escorted her down the hall again.

"I have to go to the bathroom," she murmured.

"Okay."

He stopped at the powder room near the den and looked inside. The window was small.

"Sorry. I can't close the door," he said.

"You've got to be kidding."

"I won't watch."

"Gee. Thanks."

She gave him a dark look as she strode into the bathroom. When she came out again, he motioned her down the hall. "Go through the next door. Into the den." When they were both inside, he looked around. "Sit on the sofa."

She obeyed without comment, but he felt her stiffen as he got a pair of handcuffs out of his duffel bag.

"You're not really going to do that, are you?" she whispered.

"Sorry, but I can't trust you," he said as he cuffed her left hand to an ornate wooden sofa arm.

His stomach clenched when he watched her huddle against the cushions. "I'll be right back."

First he went out to the car and unloaded his duffel bag and the electronics equipment he'd brought.

Then he moved the vehicle to the far end of the property.

When he came back, he used the bathroom, then descended to the basement, where he checked out one of the features that he remembered from his previous visits to the house. Finally, hurrying as fast as he could, he went upstairs and searched for the linen closet.

As he stood staring at the perfectly folded towels and sheets, he scrubbed his hands over his face.

Everything he was doing with Lily was wrong. He should let her go and clear out of town. But he didn't seem capable of doing the right thing, not when he'd trapped them both on a speeding train to nowhere.

With a grimace, he picked up a couple of comforters and brought them down. When he came back to the den, his gaze shot to the sofa arm. It looked like she'd been trying to wrench herself loose. But the carved post had held.

Their eyes met for a split second, and she looked

away. Before he could comment, she tipped her head toward the bedding. "What's that for?"

"Sleeping upstairs could be dangerous. If somebody comes looking for me, I could get trapped. We'll bunk down here."

"Who would come looking for you?" she asked, like she was hoping the cavalry was on the way.

"Nobody, I hope. But I'm not taking chances."

"There's nothing to prevent *me* from sleeping upstairs." She looked like she wanted to add something, then changed her mind, probably thinking better of poking a figurative stick at the dangerous beast between her and the doorway.

"I want you with me where I can keep an eye on you."

She glared at him as he spread one quilted comforter on the floor.

He unlocked the handcuff. "Lie down."

She raised her chin. "Not with you."

"I'm not going to bother you. You can close your eyes and pretend I'm not there."

"Oh, sure." Still, after considering her options, she did as he asked.

When he started to refasten the cuff to the sofa leg, she hitched in a breath. "Have mercy on me. I can't lie in one position all night.

While he thought about his alternatives, he

grabbed some pillows from the sofa and handed her one. Then he turned off the overhead light, so that only the lamp on the end table provided some illumination. It was enough to see his wife's set expression.

She propped a pillow behind her head and watched him warily as he rummaged in his duffel bag and brought out a length of rope.

He ran the rope through the handcuff loop he'd left empty, then tied both ends to his own wrist. If she tried to get away, he'd know immediately what she was doing. But the arrangement did give him the opportunity to get a little sleep.

With a disgusted look, she rocked back, flopping her head against the pillow. There was enough slack in the rope for her to roll to her side, with her back to him.

Reaching over her, he turned off the lamp, plunging the room into darkness.

As they lay next to each other, he could feel the ill will radiating off her. His mind flashed back to the early years of their marriage, when they'd always slept touching each other, her body warm and pliant in his arms. Now it felt as if he was lying next to a piece of hard, cold stone. He wanted to turn toward her and take her in his arms so he could soothe away all the tension between them.

He stayed on his own side of the makeshift bed, thinking about how many changes they'd gone through in a very short time.

A lifetime ago, she'd been angry with him for spoiling their weekend together. Then she'd been worried about him after the accident. And when he'd finally come home, it was with the cops hot on his trail.

He wanted to make everything right between them. More than right. He wanted Lily on his side. And he wanted the comfort only she could give him. But he had no idea how to accomplish that goal. What if he told her about his new talent? Would that convince her something really bad had happened at Cranesbrook?

And would she even believe him? Not without a demonstration.

The thought of working some kind of parlor trick made a wave of fatigue wash over him. Using his new skill so many times in the past few hours had exhausted him. He needed to sleep. Then in the morning, he could show her some proof of what had happened to him.

In the army, he'd learned to snatch shut-eye when he could get it. Closing his eyes, he went through one of the relaxation exercises he'd learned, then sank into an uneasy sleep.

IN HIS NIGHTMARE, Gage was cold and naked and being chased through a forest. As he ran for his life, brambles reached out and scratched his flesh. Men came crashing after him, shouting for him to stop. Without turning, he somehow saw that one of them was Tucker, the janitor from the mental hospital. Like Gage, he was naked and blood was streaming down his face. Instead of a mop, he held a gun in his hand.

"Stop. You can't escape."

"Oh, yeah?" Gage shouted. But the cold wind carried his words away.

He kept running, because that was his only option. Shots whizzed past his head and shoulders, and he braced for the impact of hot lead striking his body. If he could only make it to the safe house, he would be okay. Ahead of him he saw a stone mansion that was more like a medieval castle than a modern home.

The Wilson estate. There he would find warmth and safety. And Lily. She was waiting for him there. Probably she'd cooked him a feast in the big gourmet kitchen. But they'd eat later.

First he wanted to make love with her.

Somehow, he was no longer in the woods. He was inside the castle, lying on a big bed with his wife. He was on his back, and she was propped on her elbow, leaning over him.

She smiled down at him, then bent to stroke her lips against his cheek. He couldn't see one of her hands. Was it handcuffed or something?

He couldn't remember why. And he didn't want to think about that now. Not when she was running her fingers down his body, playing with his belt buckle, then pressing over the erection straining at the front of his slacks.

He responded with a shuddering breath.

"I want you, Gage."

The way she said his name was like the old days when they'd been so in love that they couldn't get enough of each other. He'd come home for dinner, and they'd end up in bed. Then it would be hours before they actually got around to eating the wonderful meal she'd prepared.

He closed his eyes again, because this was so much better than reality. Now he ached for her, and she had come back to him.

"You're awake," she murmured, her voice low and trembly in the darkness.

He was. The dream had transformed into reality. But still, he was afraid that the warmth and sensuality would vanish.

"Lily, don't leave me."

"I won't."

To seal the bargain she leaned closer so that her lips could slide to his mouth, pressing, urging.

He didn't need the seduction. And he didn't question what was happening between them. All he could think was that Lily had realized they belonged together, and now she was fulfilling all his pent-up longing.

The kiss was hot and urgent and familiar. She was his wife, and they had done this a thousand times, but she never failed to kindle an excitement within him that he had felt with no other woman. Yet as her tongue darted into his mouth, he sensed something below the surface of her desire, some secret emotion he should examine a little more carefully.

He might have tried to continue with that line of reasoning, but the kiss drove rational thought from his mind. Then her hand drifted over his body again, stopping at his nipples. They were hard and aching, like his erection.

She slid one hand lower, rocking her palm against that hard shaft, drowning him in a fog of sensuality. His hips moved against her hand, increasing the wonderful pressure.

He groaned as her tongue stroked his teeth, then slid along the side of his tongue. He remembered how good she was at kissing. He'd found that out on their first date.

Now she was reminding him of what he'd been missing all these weeks.

His hand slid around the back of her head so that his fingers could winnow into the blond mass. Her hair was thick and bouncy, the familiar feel of it adding to the web of sensuality.

He reached to cup her breast, cradling the soft, supple mound, his fingers stroking the hardened tip.

But she stopped his hand with shaky fingers. "Lie back. Let me do everything."

"Everything?" he asked, feeling his own grin.

"Oh, yes."

It was too dark for him to see her clearly. But every other sense was working overtime. He drank in her wonderful taste. Felt the lines of her body. Wrapped himself in her familiar scent, in the intensity of his desire for her.

No other woman had satisfied him the way she could. But he'd been so busy with the Cranesbrook job that it had been weeks since they'd made love.

Now that she was in his arms again, it was heavenly.

He might have told her to turn on the lamp so he could see her leaning over him, but she was keeping him far too occupied for independent thought.

Blood pounded hotly through his veins.

"Lily, please," he gasped.

She made a small sound of assent. With her mouth still on his, she began to unbutton his shirt, slipping her hand inside, combing through his chest hair.

"It's a little awkward trying to make love like this. I could move around better if you'd unfasten my other hand," she whispered.

"Yeah."

He hadn't told her how easy it was to get out of the rope, from his end at least. All he had to do was work the loop down his wrist and over his hand.

Quickly he freed her. "Okay?"

"Yes."

She spoke only that one syllable. But something about the low tone of her voice and the sudden tension in her body must have warned him, because he suddenly knew he was in big trouble.

Chapter Six

Gage's instincts were good. He jolted to the side, just as something hard came down with a thunk on the spot where his head had been.

Instead, a crack of agony reverberated through his shoulder.

His curse of pain echoed his wife's gasp of fear.

"What the hell?" he growled.

In the dark, he could see only shadows. But he spotted Lily jumping up and bolting for the door.

Ignoring his throbbing shoulder, he pushed himself to his feet and sprinted after her.

She had reached the hall when his good arm shot out and captured her.

With one large hand, he caught her two wrists in his. Still holding her captive, he marched her back to the sofa, then fumbled for the lamp on the end table. When he found the shade and not the metal base, he realized what had happened.

While he'd been sleeping, she'd been plotting how to get away. First she'd wiggled her way over to the lamp. The next part of her plan had been getting him to untie her. After that, she was going to bash him on the head and get the hell out of there.

His curse made her cringe.

Afraid to let go of her until he saw the lay of the land, he dragged her back to the doorway and found the wall switch. They both blinked in the sudden brightness.

"Nice try," he growled.

She looked scared, but defiant. "What did you expect me to do?" she demanded.

"Not pretend you wanted to make love with me, then try to kill me."

She raised her chin. "I wasn't trying to kill you. I just wanted to knock you out. And get away."

"You might not have intended to kill me, but it could have worked out that way if you'd left me here, bleeding into the brain."

She sucked in a breath, then went on the attack again. "Like you didn't intend to kill that janitor?"

"Nothing I did to him would have caused his death," he said.

"If you'd let me go, I wouldn't have had to hit you."

"Right," he answered, working to contain his anger. "You're stuck with me for the time being. So you might as well get used to it." He considered the recent incident. "But we have changed the equation. No way am I going to sleep next to you."

With a huffing sound, she lay down.

He attached the free cuff to the sofa arm again, being careful not to make eye contact. He wasn't feeling too good about the previous episode. He'd thought she wanted him, and all she'd been trying to do was escape.

That hurt more than the blow to his shoulder. Unfortunately, it also made him wonder again if he really was out of touch with reality. He'd read her so wrong. Of course, that had been her goal all along. She'd wanted him to think they were back together as a couple, so she'd started making love to him.

Because he was so vulnerable, he'd accepted without question what she'd seemed to be offering. Well, he'd better be on his guard now

No, stop thinking that way, he silently ordered himself. *How about rethinking your stupid decision to hold her captive?* But that would mean driving her away from the estate and finding another place to hide out, both of which were too much to tackle at the moment.

"I'll let you go in the morning," he said.

"Oh, sure."

He figured there was no use trying to convince her of his good intentions. Careful not to touch her again, he laid one of the comforters on the table near her head, in case she wanted a cover, then he took one of the pillows and the other comforter to the far side of the room and spread it on the floor.

Lying down, he wedged the pillow under his head. But now he was thinking that if Lily somehow managed to get loose, she'd tiptoe into the kitchen, get a knife and assault him.

That was ridiculous, he told himself. She didn't want to kill him. She only wanted to get away.

Right?

In the dim light, he turned his head toward her. She was lying on the sofa. Then, as if she sensed that he was watching her, she rolled to her side and drew her legs up, facing the cushions and effectively shutting him out.

As PART of his interviews, Rand had asked the Five Star employees about other jobs the company worked. He'd found out they also installed security systems, and one of the men had given him a list of installation jobs. The information provided a whole new avenue of exploration.

After taking a quick shower and changing his clothes, he sat down to call Richard, just as his phone rang.

It was his partner.

"I was just getting ready to call you," Rand said.

"About?"

"You go first."

"I've been out to Beech Grove."

"You were up early."

"Yeah. And I did find fresh bullet holes in a couple of tree trunks."

"So Darnell wasn't lying about that."

"Or he saw somebody outside taking target practice."

"Unlikely," Rand muttered.

"I've got a CSI team digging out the slugs. What did you have for me?" Richard asked.

"I've figured out a couple of locations where Darnell could be hiding out."

"Oh, yeah?"

Rand explained his theory, then said, "I'll meet you at the office, and we can plot our strategy from there."

AROUND DAWN, Gage gave up the idea of sleeping. And from the way Lily looked, he was pretty sure she hadn't slept either.

As he sat in the chair facing the sofa, he clenched and unclenched his hands.

"Want some breakfast?" he asked.

"No."

"There's instant coffee."

"No thanks."

"What, are you on a hunger strike?" he asked.

"Maybe if I pass out, you'll be forced to take me to the hospital."

"Interesting theory." He sighed. He'd started off thinking that telling his wife about his new talent was the wrong approach. Now he was sure that was the only way to get her on his side.

Unless it went the other way and he convinced her that he was a freak. But since she was already hostile, he figured he didn't have much to lose.

"Please just listen. I'm going to let you go. But first I want to tell you what I think happened at Cranesbrook. And after that."

"Do I have a choice?"

He sighed and plowed ahead. "Cranesbrook had a Defense Department contract. Maybe it's actually something that's technically illegal."

"Oh, sure," she muttered.

"Or maybe somebody there was conducting an illegal experiment, and it blew up in my face. At any rate, they're trying to cover something up, so they stowed me in Beech Grove and wouldn't let me talk to anyone. Don't you think it's a little strange that they wouldn't even let me see *you?*"

She didn't speak, so he plowed ahead.

"But I screwed up their plans by escaping, and they went into a panic. Now they're thinking if the cops kill me, I can't tell anyone about what happened."

"Do you know how insane that sounds?" she asked, then sucked in a sharp breath when she realized what she'd said.

"I can prove that they were doing something pretty strange. Wait here."

She gave a hollow laugh. "I'm handcuffed to the sofa. I'll be here when you get back."

He walked down the hall to the kitchen and picked up a stainless-steel knife and fork from the cutlery drawer.

She was looking toward the hall when he stepped into the room again. "What's that?"

"Some implements for demonstration purposes."

He handed her the knife and fork.

"What am I supposed to do with them?"

"Make sure they're solid, sturdy. See if you can bend them in your hands."

"What is this—some kind of magic act?"

"Yeah."

She tried to bend the knife and the fork, with no success, then set them down on the coffee table.

After giving the cutlery a long look, he raised his eyes to Lily again. "I ran into the lab and then there was an explosion. And I woke up in the hospital, strapped to a bed."

"You already told me that part."

"You asked me how I got loose, and I didn't want to tell you because I knew you'd think I was lying. Or worse. But I think giving you some solid evidence might help you understand what's going on."

She tried to project that she wasn't very interested in what he had to say, but he caught a subtle change in her demeanor.

"There were leather cuffs around my wrists. They were buckled tight, and I started wishing that they would loosen and they did."

"What's that supposed to mean?"

"I didn't know what it meant then. I thought I had just gotten lucky. But I got free of the restraints, and when I made it out of the building, I started running across the grounds. Did I tell you someone was shooting at me?"

Her head jerked up, but she kept her expression neutral. "So you say."

"Ask the police if they found any bullets embedded in the trees."

"How can I do that if you're holding me captive?"

Ignoring the comment, he continued. "I ran into the woods before the guy with the gun could put a bullet in my back. Only, then I came to a metal fence, and I knew I was too weak to climb over. But I pulled on the bars, and they opened up."

She made a snorting sound.

He picked up the knife and fork, then flattened his hand and held the implements balanced across his palm.

Seeing he had Lily's full attention, he focused on the utensils. But he was nervous. This wasn't like the other tests. This was in front of his wife. At first nothing happened.

When he heard Lily sigh, he clamped his lower lip between his teeth, then tried harder. Finally, something began to change. The metal started to soften so that he could slowly bend the shafts around each other while they still lay on his flattened palm.

Raising his gaze, he stared at Lily. Her eyes had gone round. "How…how did you work that trick?" she asked in a shaky voice.

He kept his own voice low and even. "With my mind."

"That's impossible."

"Yeah. It should be. But after I came to in the hospital, I found out I could do stuff nobody else can. Like I told you, that's how I got out of the cuffs."

He set the knife and fork down on the table. Feeling more confident now, he reversed the process, using his thoughts to straighten the cutlery out again. The utensils clanked against the wood surface as they assumed their former shape—only neither one of them was quite as straight as it had been before he'd twisted them.

Gingerly, with her free hand, Lily reached out and picked up the fork, testing its tensile strength and running her fingers over the metal as though she expected it to be made out of rubber.

"No trick," he said.

She put the fork down and looked at him. "And you developed that…after the lab accident?"

"Yes. I think they're worried that something strange happened to me. That's why they were holding me captive where nobody could interview me. That's why they don't want me on the loose." He'd said something similar earlier. A few minutes ago, she'd dismissed his explanation out of hand. Now she was listening.

But when she pressed against the sofa back, he

realized that his demonstration might not have had the desired effect. He'd wanted Lily to believe that he was telling the truth because he'd thought that would justify what he'd done.

At the moment it looked more like she was afraid of him.

"I'm the same guy," he assured her.

"I don't think so."

"I didn't kill anybody. I just got the hell out of that asylum."

He watched her swallow, watched her consider what she'd just seen and what he was saying.

"I'm sorry I kidnapped you," he added in a low voice. "That was a mistake."

"Yes," she answered, but she didn't sound entirely positive. "Maybe you can even consider the situation from my point of view."

When she didn't speak further, he admitted, "I've handled this wrong." He hitched in a breath. "I wanted you with me."

"Why?" she whispered.

"Because…I love you," he answered.

She stared at him. "That doesn't make sense."

"What part?" he asked.

"If you loved me, you would have considered my welfare."

"I was too needy for that," he admitted. "I'm

sorry." It was time for honesty. Way past time. "Before the explosion, I was all wound up with my job. I was a fool to be neglecting you, to neglect what we created together."

"You've picked a funny time for a heart-to-heart talk."

"I finally figured out what a jerk I've been. I hope it's not too late."

"I don't know," she whispered.

"Even if you…" He swallowed and started again. "Even if you don't feel the same about me, I hope you believe that lab accident got me exposed to a chemical that…that gave me weird powers. And I hope you believe I didn't kill that janitor."

Before she could answer, a loud noise from outside made them both jump.

"Gage Darnell, this is the police. We know you're in there. We have the house surrounded. Put down your weapons and come out with your hands in the air."

Chapter Seven

Gage went rigid. Muttering a curse, he moved toward the edge of the window, pulled the curtains aside and looked out. Five patrol cars and an unmarked were pulled up in the driveway.

Apparently the cops had been smarter—and more persistent—than he'd realized. They must have gone back through the records of Five Star looking at the past jobs his company had taken on, then come upon the Wilson estate. When they'd checked out the place, they'd found a car stolen from a parking lot in the Baltimore Inner Harbor area. And now they were outside with a bullhorn and a SWAT team.

He threw a look at Lily. Nothing was settled between them, and he had no idea what would happen now.

"What are you going to do? Use me as a shield again?" she asked.

"No."

"Why not?"

"Because this isn't two detectives showing up at our house. They have a SWAT team out there, and you could get hurt." He gave her a regretful look. "I think you were finally starting to believe me. Too bad about the cops."

Walking toward her, he held his hand near the handcuff that held her to the sofa arm, and the lock snapped open. She blinked, then pulled her hand free.

OUTSIDE, Rand and Richard stood behind their unmarked car, watching the SWAT team move into position.

They'd checked out several locations where Darnell had put in security systems. At the Wilson mansion, they'd hit pay dirt.

A car stolen from the Inner Harbor was hidden in the woods. Odds were Gage and Lily Darnell were in the house. Hopefully, the fugitive hadn't hurt his wife. But this was a tricky situation since there was no reason to assume that he was going to come out quietly.

Richard raised the bullhorn again. "This is the Maryland State Police. Gage Darnell, we have you surrounded. Come out with your hands up."

There was no answer.

"How long do we give him?" Richard asked his partner.

"I don't want the wife to get hurt."

"Did you just see the curtains move over there?" Richard asked, inclining his head slightly toward the right side of the building.

"Uh-huh."

He signaled to the leader of the SWAT team, and the man came over to confer with them.

GAGE LET GO of the curtain. The two guys in suits partially blocked by an unmarked car looked a lot like the cops who had come to his house the night before. They must have been up all night digging for information on their murder suspect.

He dragged in a breath, let it out in a rush. Then he put his life into Lily's hands and asked, "Are you willing to help me get away?"

Unable to draw in a full breath, he watched her face, watched her deciding his fate—and hers.

"Okay," she finally said.

"Thank you."

"How much time do you need?"

"If you can get me ten or fifteen minutes, that would be good."

"You have a way to get out of the house?"

"Yes."

"How?"

"It's better if you don't know."

"I'll try to buy you some time."

"I'm sorry I kidnapped you. I'm sorry I put you in danger. I should have let you go as soon as I got away from those cops."

She answered with a small nod.

He should get the hell out of there while the getting was good. Instead, he crossed to her and folded her into his arms. At first, she stood rigid, then he felt her melt against him. Now that it was too late for anything besides goodbye.

"Be careful, Gage," she whispered.

"I will."

He lowered his head and slanted his lips over hers, and she responded with a frantic urgency that made his heart leap. Passion flared between them. Real passion. Not the charade she'd manufactured last night.

He wanted to keep holding her, keep kissing her. He wanted to tear off her clothes and his, and drag her down to the carpet so he could show her how much he needed her. But that was impossible now.

They were out of time. Maybe forever.

But at least he knew she was willing to help him, if this wasn't another one of her tricks. He couldn't entirely discount the terrible possibility that she was going to run to the front door and let the cops in the moment he left the room.

He set her away from him and her eyes blinked open, looking dazed.

He'd gotten her into this mess, and he had to think about her safety above his own. "You need a white flag," he whispered.

"I'll find something. You go on."

"Thanks," he said, meaning it from the bottom of his heart.

Knowing his only option was to trust her, he dashed across the room and looked at the duffel bag and the box he'd brought in the night before. He was going to be on foot, and he had the choice of taking the electronics equipment or the personal items.

He scooped up the equipment, then dashed for the basement stairs.

LILY COULD HEAR Gage pounding down the steps to the lower level. There must be some way out down there, some exit she didn't know about. Up until a few minutes ago, they'd been kidnapper and captive. And she'd been desperate enough to play a terrible trick on him while he was sleeping.

She wasn't proud of that. But she knew he wasn't proud of putting her in danger, either.

At least, she'd started to think that when he'd changed tactics and begun talking to her like the Gage Darnell she remembered.

He'd sounded sincere. He'd kissed her like he meant it. And he'd just put his life in her hands.

She knew one thing for sure: She wanted to continue the conversation with him, and if the cops took him into custody, that would be impossible.

Without wasting any more time, she dashed up the steps to the second floor and ran down the hall, looking into the bathrooms and bedrooms. The first white piece of cloth she saw was a towel hanging in one of the bathrooms. She snatched it off the rack, then stood clutching the terry cloth, wondering what she was going to do.

She'd been convinced that Gage was crazy and dangerous.

Until he'd pulled that trick with the knife and fork.

She'd held the utensils herself and knew they were perfectly solid. It seemed that he'd been telling her the truth. He'd acquired a paranormal ability when he'd gotten caught in that accident at Cranesbrook.

Which led to another question. Did the people at Cranesbrook actually know what the explosion had done to him—or were they trying to figure it out?

He'd said he hadn't killed the janitor. He'd said that somebody at Beech Grove had shot at him when he'd tried to escape.

She hadn't known whether to believe any of that. Now she felt that the evidence was on his side. Or maybe she *wanted* to believe.

She might have mulled over that point if she hadn't had a more pressing problem—saving her own life.

She'd told Gage she would help him get away, but she had seen too many news accounts of innocent bystanders and hostages getting shot by accident. If she didn't want to end up as a statistic, she'd better do this right.

What would protect her while giving Gage the best chance of getting away?

After debating for a few moments, she went back to the nearest bedroom, where she found a telephone on the bedside table.

Snatching up the receiver, she dialed 911.

"What is your emergency?" a female voice asked.

"This is Lily Darnell. I'm at the Wilson estate on Brockbridge Road. I'm being held hostage, and there's a SWAT team outside. I want to surrender. Can you put me in touch with the officer in charge outside?"

"A hostage situation?" the woman asked.

"Yes. It's imperative that I talk to the officer in charge. I'm at the Wilson estate on Brockbridge Road," she repeated, then looked at the telephone. "The number is 410-555-2233. I'll be waiting for them to call me."

She replaced the receiver and sat down on the bed with her hands clasped tightly in her lap. Long seconds ticked by, and she wondered if her tactic was going to work.

Finally, the phone rang.

GAGE OPENED what looked like a closet door. But nothing was on the other side besides a metal gate. He'd checked to make sure that the tunnel was available as an escape route, but he hadn't done anything about the rusty lock.

Holding the padlock in his hand, he peered down at the keyhole, thinking that he should have taken care of this last night. But when he'd arrived, he'd been congratulating himself on his cleverness. He'd considered this escape route as extra insurance. He shouldn't have been so arrogant.

As he turned his attention back to the lock, he thought about the interior workings. This was like starting on a car or a boat, he told himself. But as he tried to make the mechanism snap open, he found that it wasn't quite so easy. The rusted interior resisted his efforts.

Damn.

Upstairs, he heard the phone ring. What the hell was that? One ring. Then it stopped. Had Lily answered?

Was she about to turn him in? Or had the cops figured out how to make a call to the mansion?

"HELLO?" Lily said into the phone.

"This is Randall McClellan of the Maryland State Police. To whom am I speaking?"

"This is Lily Darnell. Are you one of the officers who was at my house last night?"

"Yes."

"Thank God you've found me."

"Are you all right, Mrs. Darnell?"

She took a deep breath before answering. "Yes. I'm in one of the upstairs bedrooms. I'd go to the window, but I don't want to end up getting shot."

"You won't be," he assured her quickly.

"I've watched enough news accounts of hostage situations to know I'd better be careful."

"Okay." There was a pause on the other end of the line. Apparently he had covered the phone receiver, because she could hear only muffled words while he conferred with someone else.

"Is your husband willing to surrender?" McClellan asked when he came back on the line.

"I don't think so. But he's willing to let me go."

"Okay."

"What should I do?"

"Do you have a white flag?"

"Yes."

"Go to the front door."

"How can I be sure I won't get shot? Can you come up the walk and meet me?"

He made a harsh sound. "How can I be sure I won't get shot?"

"Good question. I guess we have to work something out. I'm going to hang up."

"Don't!" the cop said urgently.

"I'm going to go down and find a portable phone. Give me your number, so I can call you back directly."

"Darnell is letting you walk around the house?"

"Yes." Without further explanation, she hung up and went downstairs.

GAGE SENT his mind into the lock again, scraping away the rust. When the mechanism finally clicked, he felt a flood of relief.

Flashlight in hand, he stepped into a dark tunnel. It was dank and musty, and he wanted to get out of there as soon as possible, but he took the time to relock the gate behind him before starting down the passageway.

Savagely, he squelched the impulse to run. He'd never been in here before, and he didn't want to stumble into some booby trap left over from the bootlegging days when this secret route had been constructed. So he forced himself to go slowly, counting his paces as he went.

Playing the light in front of him and along the wall, he kept walking forward. He was a hundred and twenty paces from the gate when the flashlight beam hit a wooden door.

Like the gate in the basement, the door was locked. Shining the light over the vertical surface, he found the lock and fingered it. Large and old-fashioned, it probably hadn't been used in years, but he sent his mind into the inner workings, just as he had at the other end. Once again the rust proved to be a barrier.

The house seemed far away now. What was Lily doing? Were the cops already inside?

"Stay safe," he whispered, knowing that he was secretly listening for the sound of shots from above.

LILY PICKED UP the portable phone in the little office off the kitchen. She glanced at the clock and waited another minute before dialing McClellan, stalling to give Gage time to get away.

He answered on the first ring. "Mrs. Darnell? Are you all right?"

"Yes. And I'd like to come out. If we can do that without my getting shot."

"You have my word on that."

She gave a harsh laugh. "Okay. I'm going to walk to the front of the house. I'll stand back from the window, but I want to see you in the driveway."

"I'll be there."

"Tell the SWAT team to put their weapons down. Then raise your hands and step out where I can see you."

The volume was turned up loud enough for Richard to hear the conversation.

Rand felt his partner's hand on his shoulder. "You're not going to do it, are you?"

"If course I'm going to do it."

"This could be a trick. The bastard could be planning to shoot you."

"I don't think so."

"You're willing to bet your life on that?"

"Yes."

Rand raised his voice. "Red light. Red light.

Put your weapons down. Mrs. Darnell, the hostage, is coming out."

The leader of the SWAT team hesitated, then ordered his men to stand down.

Feeling like a moving target, Rand stepped from behind the unmarked and into the circle of the driveway. Then he raised his hands above his head and took several steps toward the front door.

When it opened, he tensed.

Somebody poked a white flag outside. Seconds later, a figure stepped onto the porch. It was Lily Darnell, clutching a bath towel.

She took several steps toward him, wavering on unsteady feet. He rushed forward and steadied her, then led her down the driveway and behind the unmarked.

"You're all right?" he asked.

"Yes."

"Where's Darnell?"

"I don't know."

"What do you mean?"

"I woke up, and he was missing."

"You're saying you're alone in the house?"

"Yes."

Rand struggled not to mutter a curse. His eyes focused on Mrs. Darnell, he asked, "If he's not here, why did you go through that elaborate phone call? Why did you let me think he was still there? You were talking like he'd given you permission to speak to me."

She dragged in a breath and huffed it out. "Like I told you, I was worried about getting hurt. You were assuming he'd be there, so I acted like you'd expect me to act. It's a relief to know I'm still in one piece."

"And now you're saying the house is empty?" Rand clarified.

"As far as I know."

Rand turned from the woman. She seemed shaken but unhurt. Still, he didn't exactly trust her.

Richard came forward. "Should I send the SWAT team in?"

"Yeah. But advise them to use extreme caution."

GAGE LOCKED the door behind him. Stepping into the woods, he shouldered the box of equipment that he'd brought from home. It was heavy, he wanted to ditch it, but many items would be difficult to replace, since he'd designed them himself. So he clamped his arm around the box and jogged through the woods.

He'd thought he was safe at the Wilson estate. Now he was rethinking his plans.

Up ahead he saw a road. He stayed away from

it and wove his way through the trees until a house came into view through the still-green leaves. And a car. A late-model Ford.

He needed transportation. But when he approached the vehicle, a large dog leaped out of the woods and came straight for him.

"HOW LONG have you been alone?" the detective asked Lily. They were seated in the rear of the unmarked car.

"I'm not sure."

When he continued to stare at her, she raised her chin. "I woke up in the downstairs den. When I went to sleep the night before, Gage was with me. When I got up he wasn't there."

"What time was that?"

She looked down at her hands, and he was pretty sure she was going to tell him a lie. "Thirty minutes ago."

"You slept late."

"I was exhausted."

"You could sleep when you thought you were in extreme danger?"

"I never thought I was in extreme danger. I knew Gage wouldn't hurt me."

"Why did he kidnap you?"

She swallowed and raised her eyes toward his.

Giving him a direct look, she said, "He told me he had to get away. He said he was innocent and he'd been framed. He said that if you took him into custody, he'd never be able to prove his innocence."

The sincerity in her eyes argued that she was telling the truth. At least as far as she knew it. Darnell certainly wouldn't have told her he was a murderer. Still, Rand was pretty sure she wasn't giving him the whole story.

"Why did you wait for half an hour to call for help?"

"I didn't know if I was alone in the house. I didn't know if it was some kind of trick. If maybe Gage was waiting to see what I would do. But when he didn't show up, I figured it was okay to talk to you."

Rand looked up to see his partner standing in the doorway. Excusing himself, he exited the car and walked toward the house, nodding at a nearby officer to watch Mrs. Darnell.

"I take it the SWAT team didn't find him," he said to his partner.

"Right. As far as we can tell, the house is empty. I found a pair of handcuffs in the den. One end is still attached to the sofa arm. So he must have freed her at some point."

"Yeah. The question is when?"

"Also, there's something interesting in the basement. Apparently somebody put in a tunnel that leads to the woods at the edge of the property. There's a gate in the basement and a door at the other end. We had to bust through both of them. A door hid the gate, but it was open."

"You think he went out that way?"

"I think it's likely."

"But he unlocked the gate and the door and locked them again?"

"I think so."

"Why would he do that?"

"To throw us off his trail. And slow us down."

Rand nodded.

Richard continued, "Besides the car he came in, there are two more vehicles in the garage—an SUV and an Acura. I think he's on foot."

"There could have been a third vehicle on the property."

"I've contacted the owners. They say they left only two cars here. So we have to ask ourselves if he had time to plan an escape, why didn't he drive?"

Rand considered the implications. "Maybe when we arrived, Darnell and his wife cooked something up. She stalled us long enough for him to get down the tunnel. You've sent men into the woods?"

"Uh-huh."

"Why would she do that? It looked like she was pretty scared when he hustled her out of their house."

"They got cozy during the night?" Richard theorized.

"A possibility."

"Whatever happened, he can't get far on foot."

"Let's hope not."

"Do you think we can get the truth out of the wife?"

Rand tightened his jaw. "I'm sure as hell going to try."

Chapter Eight

Gage sprinted for the car. To his everlasting relief, the vehicle was unlocked. He leaped inside, then pulled the door closed seconds before the dog reached the side of the car.

It continued to bark, standing on its hind legs and snapping its jaw at him through the window, but it couldn't get inside and chew his leg off.

LILY LOOKED UP as the detective came back into the car. His face was set in grim lines, and she suspected he had acquired some new information.

A bolt of fear flashed through her. Had they captured Gage? Killed him? She ached to ask, but she couldn't give away that she was worried.

"We've found a tunnel in the basement," he said.

"And?"

"It looks like your husband escaped that way."

"Okay."

"When did he leave, Mrs. Darnell?"

"I told you, I don't know. I was sleeping. When I woke up, he was gone."

The detective regarded her with unblinking eyes. "You're sure he wasn't here when we arrived?"

She kept her own gaze steady and hoped she wasn't giving away her lie. "Yes."

He looked as though he doubted her story. Well, too bad. He couldn't prove anything.

She threw him a question. "Gage said someone shot at him when he was escaping from Beech Grove. He said you'd find bullets embedded in tree trunks. Did you check on that?"

The detective looked uncomfortable. "Yes."

"And you found the bullets?"

He nodded.

"What do you make of that?"

"There's no proof the bullets were fired yesterday."

"Why should *anybody* be shooting on the Beech Grove grounds?"

"I don't know," he admitted.

"Well, while you figure it out, I'd like to go home and decompress."

"After we go down to the State Police barracks so you can press kidnapping charges."

She'd forgotten about that part of the equation. "I'm not planning to press charges."

"Why not?"

Struggling to stay calm and in control, she waited a beat before answering. "I think Gage was framed. I think he was desperate to prove his innocence. That's why he had to get away from you."

"So you were willing to help him escape?"

"I didn't say that."

"I can arrest you as an accessory after the fact in a murder case."

LISTENING FOR the sound of sirens, Gage drove a few miles, then turned onto another residential street. Scanning the houses, he found another one where the owner was away and exchanged the Ford for a beat-up Toyota. After that, he stopped at another house and switched license plates. With any luck, he could drive the Toyota for a while without fear of getting caught.

That stopped him short. Without fear?

Who was he kidding?

He wasn't going to be free of fear until he figured out how to clear his name of the murder charge that Dr. Morton had stuck on him.

Of course, Morton might not be the one who had come up with the idea. Maybe he was being paid by someone else. Sid Edmonston, Martin

Kelso and Nelson Ulrich had all been on the scene the afternoon of the explosion. So had Evan Buckley, for that matter. And Hank Riddell had been hanging around the hospital, presumably to watch both Gage and Vanderhoven.

Back at the lab, it had looked as if Kelso had been unconscious, but that could be a trick. Really, any of them could be working with Morton. Or Morton could be working for *them*. Or someone else from the lab could have been doing illegal experiments-using the lab's resources for his own purposes. Like what if one of the employees was cooking up designer drugs?

Gage snorted. It was far-fetched. But at least it was a possibility.

He might have suspected Vanderhoven. He'd never liked the little twit. But Vanderhoven had been caught in the same explosion as Gage and was now in the loony bin.

Which was where Gage would have been if he hadn't escaped. And unless he stayed free, he wouldn't find out what was going on. Unfortunately, staying out of the clutches of the law meant engaging in some more criminal activity. With a murder charge hanging over his head. Maybe even kidnapping, if Lily pressed charges.

Maybe they'd force her to do that in exchange for her own freedom.

The whole situation made his stomach clench. He didn't want to do anything else illegal, but he needed money, and clothing, since he'd abandoned his duffel bag at the Wilson estate. So he stopped at another ATM and used his convenient talent to withdraw five hundred dollars.

LILY STARED at the detective. After dropping his "accessory after the fact" bombshell, he leaned back and waited for her response.

She felt as if a fifty-pound weight was sitting on her chest, but she struggled to look calm as she lifted her chin, calling his bluff. "Detective Rand, I don't appreciate being threatened. If you want to arrest me, then go ahead and do it."

The detective gave her a long look, as though he was considering several alternatives that she wasn't going to like. He made her wait thirty nerve-wracking seconds before saying, "That may not be to our best advantage."

She eased out the breath that she hadn't realized she was holding. "I'm glad to hear that."

"It would be to *your* advantage to cooperate with us."

"I am," she lied.

He sighed. "Don't leave town."

"I wasn't planning to," she answered automatically. She didn't really know what her next move was going to be beyond going home and trying to catch some sleep.

When she realized she was clutching her hands in her lap, she deliberately relaxed them. "Can you tell me any more about the explosion at Cranesbrook?" she asked.

"No," he answered, then shot her a question of his own. "Was Five Star doing a good job at Cranesbrook?"

"Of course."

"You know that for a fact?"

"Gage was putting in a lot of overtime. He wasn't slacking off on the job."

"What about his partner, Brayden Sloane?"

"He wouldn't sit back and let things drift along, either. They formed the company because they had the same values and the same work ethic."

"Then how did somebody get through security and sabotage the lab?"

"Maybe it was an inside job," she answered.

McClellan didn't comment either way.

"At least consider that possibility."

"Whose side are you on?"

"Gage's."

"Oh, yeah."

She dropped her gaze, realizing too late that he'd tricked her into giving her feelings away. Which meant it was dangerous to keep sitting here with this cop from the Maryland State Police. She'd been up all night, and the longer she continued this discussion, the more likely it was that she'd make another mistake. Like, for example, what if she slipped up and talked about his amazing new talent?

"Can you give me a ride home?" she asked.

"I'd like to talk to you some more."

She sagged back against the seat as if she was calling on her last drop of strength, which wasn't so far from the truth. "I'm not up to it now." She almost added that she hadn't slept a wink the night before. Then she remembered that she'd claimed to be asleep when Gage had left. She'd caught herself before she'd screwed up, but she wasn't sure how long she could keep up any kind of charade since lying had never been her strong suit.

Giving the detective her best damsel-in-distress look, she asked, "Please, I need a ride. Or I can call a cab and pay when I get home, since I don't have my purse."

He waited a beat before saying, "I can give you a ride. But are you sure you're not willing to tell us what really happened here?"

She fought not to break into hysterical laughter. Gage wasn't the only one in danger. If she told the cops about Gage's new talent, she was the one who was likely to end up in the local mental hospital.

Cutting off that thought, she said, "Let's go."

After a moment, the cop slid behind the wheel and pulled away.

Last night, driving to the Wilson estate had seemed to take an eternity. Now she spent another eternity sitting quietly with her head thrown back and her eyes closed in Rand McClellan's unmarked car.

When they finally pulled into her driveway, she struggled not to breathe out a sigh of relief.

"Are you sure you won't change your mind and level with me?" he asked as he pulled to a stop in the driveway.

"I have," she said. Even to her own ears, the protestation sounded like a blatant fabrication.

With a shake of his head, he reached into his breast pocket, pulled out a card and handed it to her. "Call me if you change your mind."

As she crossed the porch, her steps faltered, but when she reached the front door and turned the knob, it opened.

Wheeling, she gestured to the cop, who was

still watching her from the open window of the unmarked car. "Thanks for not locking the door."

He flushed, and she felt bad about the sarcasm. It was a cheap shot.

"We were a little busy last night."

"Saves me the trouble of getting the spare key from around back," she tossed over her shoulder as she stepped into the house and carefully closed and locked the door behind her.

The first thing she did was inspect every room to make sure nobody was inside. Next she checked the locks on all the doors and windows. Finally, she walked into the kitchen on unsteady legs and filled the kettle.

While she waited for the water to boil, she looked around at her familiar surroundings. She'd fixed up the kitchen just the way she wanted it when they moved into this house.

New counters. A work island. A professional stove and refrigerator. Nothing as grand as at the Wilson estate but a couple of cuts above the usual home kitchen.

They'd taken out a loan for the upgrades, and Gage hadn't complained; he knew how much she loved to cook and fool around designing new recipes. All he'd wanted was a shop in the garage where he could work on his electronics inventions.

That was one of the things they had in common. The love of experimenting. Only their areas of expertise were different. She had great food sense, and he was an electronics genius.

When the kettle whistled, she fixed herself a cup of Irish Breakfast tea with milk and sugar—the way her grandmother would have done—and took it into the living room, where she dropped into Gage's favorite leather chair that sat facing the entertainment center. All the comforts of modern life.

Yet life here hadn't been right for a long time. She'd blamed Gage for staying down at Cranesbrook, but their problems weren't all his fault. They'd both been caught up in the rat race of work and they'd neglected the marriage.

She thought about the way Gage had kissed her early in the morning when she'd come on to him, and once again she felt a pang of regret at the tactic she'd chosen. She'd been desperate to get away. In response, Gage had been tender and sexy, totally into what they were doing. It was so clear he'd wanted to make love to her the way they had in the old days.

And what about her? She'd been pretending to be as wrapped up in him, all while she was really plotting to hit him over the head, escape and call the cops.

With a small sound, she lowered her head to her hands.

Tears gathered behind her closed eyes, and her shoulders began to shake.

She'd been making love with him for all the wrong reasons, and now the tactic seemed despicable.

Thank God the ploy hadn't worked, because Gage would be in jail—and unable to prove that he wasn't a murderer.

That thought sent a fresh wave of misery crashing over her.

She should have trusted her husband, not the wild story Dr. Morton had spun. Unfortunately, she'd been trained to trust doctors.

But she'd forgotten something fundamental during the hours of anxiety after the kidnapping. Until the moment when Gage had taken her captive, he had been the most honest man she'd ever known. Totally on the side of the law. He was the kind of guy who added up the check in a restaurant, and if it was wrong in the management's favor, he would pay the difference.

In this day and age, that had astonished her. But it was only one of the qualities that had attracted her to Gage Darnell in the first place.

They'd met at the restaurant where she was on

the lunch shift and he was installing a security system. She'd given him some meals while he'd been working. Then one day her shift had ended just as he was finishing up for the day, and he'd asked her if she wanted to go get a cup of coffee.

That was how it had all started.

She'd lived in Philadelphia all her life—except for her years in culinary school in Hyde Park, New York. And she'd been so impressed with Gage's background in the Special Forces. He'd lived in a country that was nothing like his own, and he had some amazing stories to tell. Like the time he and Bray had walked into an ambush and only gotten out because they'd dived into a drainage ditch.

She'd gotten him talking about some of the good things that had happened in the war zone. Like how he and the other guys had bought school supplies for some kids in Afghanistan and about how he'd helped train foreign troops in security procedures.

But the stories were just the surface. It was the man behind them that had interested her.

She knew he was conscientious and that he drove himself to the point of exhaustion. Unfortunately, that had turned out to be one of their recent problems. She should have forced him to slow down and relax a little. But she had known how important it was for him to be financially independent.

Gage's childhood had been very different from hers. Her parents had given her everything—too much, really. Riding lessons. Dance lessons. A private school. A swimming pool off the terrace.

And they'd thought it was cute when she wanted to help out the cook in the kitchen. Of course that had changed when she'd announced her plans for culinary school.

Gage's father had left the family several times. His mom had been too exhausted trying to make ends meet to pay much attention to her five kids, of whom Gage was the youngest.

The two girls had married young and moved away. One of his brothers was in jail. The other was in a dead-end job. And Mrs. Darnell had died of breast cancer in her fifties.

It was a sad story, and Lily had vowed to make the rest of Gage's life very different.

But after Five Star had taken that Cranesbrook contract, she'd felt as though she was losing him.

She made a small sound of distress. Gage had been so excited about getting the job at Cranesbrook. And look where it had gotten him. Charged with murder and running for his life.

But somebody else was really responsible. Now that she was thinking straight, she was sure of her husband's innocence.

She and Gage desperately needed to finish the conversation the cops had interrupted. On the other hand, she'd be a fool not to assume that the police weren't watching her. If she figured out where Gage had gone, she'd be leading the authorities right to him.

So she was going to have to be very careful if she didn't want to make things worse for him.

RAND HEADED BACK to the Wilson estate to pick up his partner. Discouraged but determined not to waste the trip to Baltimore, they stopped at the Five Star home office, which had apparently been set up more for utility than show, although the conference room did boast state-of-the-art media equipment for sales presentations.

A woman named Peggy Olson ran the office. She was in her fifties with bleached-blond hair pulled into a bun, red lipstick and a cardigan.

She looked up when they came in. "Can I help you?"

Rand introduced himself and his partner, and they both offered their credentials.

She sighed. "I've been expecting you. And I want you to know right off that Gage Darnell couldn't have murdered anyone."

"You're sure of that?"

"If you knew Gage, you'd agree with me."

"You must have missed the new account of him kidnapping his wife."

"But it appears she didn't press charges."

Rand sighed, knowing he'd have to dump a murder victim on her desk to get her to change her opinion of Darnell.

"Do you have any idea where Darnell might have gone?"

"None."

"What about Brayden Sloane?"

"I have no idea where he is, either."

"Was either of them in any kind of trouble?" Richard asked.

"No. They were both great guys. Hard workers. Good bosses."

"Can you give us some background on them? Where did they meet?"

"The Special Forces. And they both had excellent records," she added.

"They were discharged at the same time?"

"Brayden got out first and worked for a couple of security companies. When Gage was discharged, they started up Five Star and hired me to run the office."

Switching topics, Richard asked. "What are you going to do now?"

"Run the operation until Gage and Bray come back."

"Doing what?" Rand asked.

"We're still monitoring homes and offices with our security systems. And we have security men at some other installations."

"So you can meet your payroll?" Richard asked.

"Of course," she snapped.

From her defensive tone he figured that the financial picture at Five Star wasn't so rosy with the two owners missing.

They talked for a few more minutes, but it was apparent that Ms. Olson couldn't or wouldn't give them any more information about Darnell. Rand left his card and told her to contact him if she heard from either Darnell or Sloane, but he doubted that she would comply.

"So now I guess we're going to Cranesbrook," Richard said as they got back in the car.

Rand nodded. "I'd like a look at Darnell's medical records."

"Not without his written permission."

GAGE COULD have taken off for anywhere in the U.S., Canada or Mexico. With his new talent, he would have no trouble getting money. He could hide out in some tropical paradise or mountain retreat and make a new life for himself. Maybe he could even send for Lily—if he could make sure she didn't lead the cops to him. He indulged in that fantasy for about ten minutes, then yanked himself back to reality.

He was never going to live any kind of normal life until he cleared himself of the trumped-up murder charges.

So he selected a battered pickup truck from a lot where vehicles were being held for evidence in police cases. The way the courts worked, nobody would notice for a couple of months.

His plan was to drive back to the Eastern Shore, but he took the long way around, heading into the mountains and the small city of Hagerstown, Maryland. It was a working-class community with plenty of thrift shops.

After stopping in a drugstore for sunglasses and hair dye, he rented a room at a trucker's motel and turned his hair midnight-black. Then he inspected his face in the mirror. He hadn't shaved in three days, which gave him a good start on a beard.

At one of the thrift shops he'd bought worn jeans and some plaid shirts he wouldn't be caught dead in under ordinary circumstances, hoping that when he got back to St. Stephens, he could pass for one of the watermen who made their living from the bay.

Work boots and a baseball cap with the logo of a tractor supply store completed the disguise. It wasn't great, but he hoped it would do. Because he knew the only way he could prove his innocence was to do some investigating on his own.

AN HOUR and a half after leaving Five Star headquarters, Rand pulled the unmarked to a stop in front of the Cranesbrook gates.

A man wearing a blue-and-gray uniform with an Ace Security patch on the left shoulder came smartly out of a small guardhouse and inquired about their business.

When Rand passed over his Maryland State Police credentials, the guard inspected them carefully, then threw a switch that unlocked the gate.

Before proceeding through, Rand asked, "You new here?"

"Yes, sir."

"I thought Five Star Security had the contract."

"All I know is that we came on board a couple of days ago."

"Okay."

As they drove toward the administration building, Richard muttered, "Fast work."

"Yeah."

They pulled into a visitor's space, then got out. As soon as they gave their names to the receptionist, they were ushered into the office of the president.

Sidney Edmonston stood and came around his desk. "Detective McClellan, Detective Francis. Good to see you again."

They'd met briefly the day Darnell had broken out of the loony bin. Now they were back for some more information.

"Can Mary Ann get you anything to drink?" he asked when the secretary had ushered them into his plush office.

"No, thank you."

Edmonston was tall and thin with a fringe of dark hair around the edges of his high, bald head. He was wearing a crisp white shirt and a navy-blue suit that looked custom-tailored.

The executive unbuttoned his jacket and sat down again behind his wide desk, his body language suggesting that he liked having the barrier between himself and the cops.

Rand took out a notebook. "What can you tell us about the day of the accident?" he asked.

Edmonston sat with his hands clasped in his lap. To steady himself, Rand wondered.

"We had a security breach at the facility."

When they both remained silent, the executive continued, "A break-in at Lab 7 followed by an explosion. I already gave you that information."

"We're conducting a murder investigation now," Rand snapped. "So you need to start over with us. What is the nature of the work at the lab?"

"We have a government contract."

"For what?"

"I'm afraid that's classified."

"What branch of the government?" Richard interjected.

"The Defense Department."

Rand wrote that down.

"That's why we hired what we thought was a top security outfit. Five Star came highly recommended. But it's apparent they failed to protect us. Somebody got into Lab 7 and sabotaged the place."

"So you had a security breach and you called in Darnell and Sloane."

He hesitated. "Well, they came running over from the security office when they heard the alarm."

"And what happened then?" Rand asked, thinking that it would be easier to pull the guy's teeth than to get him to give up information.

"There was an explosion and a chemical discharge."

"Was Darnell the only one affected?"

"Wes Vanderhoven, one of our lab technicians, was caught in the explosion as well. He was also taken to Beech Grove and he's still there. Brayden Sloane was also in the lab. As you know, he's disappeared. And Dr. Martin Kelso, one of our managers, was in the lobby area. He'd been assaulted, but he's recovered."

"He's back to work?"

"Well, part-time."

"And you haven't heard anything from Sloane since the day of the accident?"

"No. I was hoping the police might get a line on him."

The comment sounded like a criticism, and Rand shifted in his seat. "We haven't been working that part of the case." Taking control of the interview again, he asked, "What will the security records show for the period before the break-in?" Rand tried.

"That Five Star was doing a good job!" Edmonston snapped. "But that doesn't prove anything. They could have been keeping up a front."

"Mmm-hmm," Richard muttered.

Edmonston gave him a sharp look but didn't comment.

"We'd like to see the lab where the accident occurred," Rand said.

"It's sealed until we check the level of toxicity."

A good way to keep people out, Rand thought. "Then we'd like to interview some of the other employees."

"Which ones?"

"Martin Kelso. And Nelson Ulrich, your Research Director."

"I've already talked to Ulrich and Kelso. They don't know anything."

Oh great, they'd coordinated their stories.

"Nevertheless, speaking to them would be useful," Rand said. "And I'm sure you must have security cameras at the lab."

"Of course."

"We'd like those tapes. And the security logs."

"I'll want all that material back."

"It won't be available immediately. We have to check it in as evidence. And we may need it for trial," Rand explained patiently.

They spent another twenty unproductive minutes with Edmonston then went back to the outer office, where a guard was waiting to escort them to the lab.

Kelso had been making a check of the labs when an unknown assailant had come at him from behind and hit him on the head. He had blacked out and come to in the hospital.

Ulrich had been on the scene outside the lab when the security men had arrived. But his story matched Edmonston's. Big surprise. And he was equally critical of Five Star.

Rand and Richard didn't discuss their thoughts on the case until they'd driven out of the Cranesbrook compound.

"Helpful bunch," Richard observed.

Rand slapped his palms against the steering wheel. "They're hiding something and I want to know what."

"Maybe they're testing something illegal at the lab and that secret government contract is a cover."

"Or they were really the ones who were negligent, and now they're blaming it on Five Star."

"Or the security guys and Edmonston had some kind of illegal agreement and it got cocked up."

"Yeah," Rand agreed.

"Or Kelso faked his own accident, so he wouldn't look guilty of anything."

Richard sighed. "We'd better keep digging."

They headed back to the office with a stop at one of the coffee shops in town for some French roast that was a hundred times better than the sludge that came from the pot in the office.

As soon as they had checked in the security tape as evidence, they took it to a viewing room.

It showed what looked like routine activity at the lab—up until a few minutes before the alleged break-in. Then the screen simply went blue.

Which was the same color as the air around them when Rand and Richard finished cursing.

"Just great," Richard muttered.

"Somebody doesn't want us to find out what happened."

"I'm beginning to like the inside-job theory more and more."

"Yeah. The question is—how does it relate to the Hillman murder?"

"We'll find a connection if we keep digging."

Rand wished he could be as sure. "Do you think the Defense Department will tell us what Cranesbrook was working on at the lab?" he wondered aloud.

"My opinion, no. But it doesn't hurt to ask."

As HE DROVE back to the Eastern Shore, Gage made some plans. His first stop was going to be the home of Hank Riddell, the guy who had been keeping tabs on him at Beech Grove. He'd get what he could out of Riddell, then work on Evan Buckley, the man on his security staff whom he'd been on the verge of firing. Riddell was definitely involved in some way. And the more Gage thought about it, the more sure he was that Buckley was in on the conspiracy.

Conspiracy. Yeah, right. Was it really up at that level?

He didn't know much about Hank Riddell, but he was pretty tuned in to Buckley. The guy was twenty-eight and still lived with his parents in Cambridge, the next town over. He had bought a honking big motorcycle recently and he'd worn some expensive snakeskin boots to work. It would be interesting to find out where he'd gotten the money.

He stopped to look up the street addresses of both men in a gas-station phone book, then ate at a crab-cake joint while he waited for dark.

When he drove past Riddell's small clapboard house on the outskirts of town, there were no lights. The blinds were closed, and the lawn looked like it was a week past mowing. When he rang the bell, nobody answered. He was standing on the sidewalk in front when a man and woman came by pushing a baby stroller.

Figuring this was as good a time as any to test his disguise, he said, "Excuse me. I'm an old friend of Hank's. I thought I'd drop in, but he doesn't seem to be home."

"No. He's been gone for over a week," the woman confirmed. "I saw him come out with a suitcase."

"He's on a trip?"

The couple exchanged glances. "I think he told Mark Carter—" the man pointed toward the house to the left of Riddell's "—his next-door neighbor, that he was going to be staying on the Cranesbrook campus."

"Cranesbrook? What's that?" Gage asked, like he'd never heard of the place.

"It's the big research lab where he works. Apparently he's on some kind of special assignment, and they need him there 24/7."

"Uh-huh," Gage answered. "Thanks for the info."

He climbed back into his truck and drove away, careful not to curse until he was out of earshot.

A special assignment? And what would that be, exactly? First he'd been assigned to Beech Grove. Now he was inside the locked Cranesbrook gates.

Strike one, Gage thought. But he could still get some answers out of Buckley. Struggling not to roar down the highway, he headed for Cambridge, but as soon as he reached the Buckley house, his spider senses started tingling. Something was wrong.

Chapter Nine

Gage drove slowly past the Buckley house. A lot of cars were parked along the street near the two-story shingled residence. As he watched, an older couple came up the sidewalk toward the house, the woman carrying a casserole dish. Either the Buckleys were having a party or something bad had happened. Gage remembered that old Mr. Buckley was in bad health. Perhaps he had died.

After finding a parking space down the block, Gage got out and walked up the sidewalk, falling into step just behind a young man and woman who were also bringing food.

His disguise had worked for the brief encounter outside Riddell's house. Emboldened, he said, "Can I join you?"

The woman stopped and turned toward him. "You were a friend of Evan's?"

Gage noted the past tense. Somehow, he wasn't even shocked. This fit perfectly into the way things were going.

"I just got back in town, so I don't know what happened."

"Such a tragedy," the woman said. "He was riding his motorcycle out on the river road, and somebody plowed into him then left him lying there and roared away."

"They didn't find him until morning," the man added.

Gage eyed the dish the woman was carrying. "Where are my manners? I should bring something. I didn't think of that until just now."

"You don't have to. I'm sure Grace and Harold will be glad to see you.

"No. I want to do something," Gage insisted. "You go along, and I'll be back in a few minutes, after I stop at the grocery store."

He turned and walked rapidly back to his car, climbed in and drove away.

So Evan Buckley was dead. It could be an unfortunate coincidence, but Gage didn't think so. He'd bet that Buckley knew something. Either he'd been in on what went down at the lab or he'd picked up some information that had gotten him killed. Had he been dumb enough to try blackmail?

Gage cursed under his breath. So much for getting some answers tonight.

"ANYTHING ON Mrs. Darnell?" Rand asked.

Richard shook his head. "She stayed in the house all day after you took her home, then went to work in the evening like nothing out of the ordinary had happened."

"She's got moxie."

"Too bad for us."

"How did Darnell get her to switch sides?"

"I wish I knew."

"We've got an APB out on him. And we've got her under surveillance. If he communicates with her, we're in a position to nab him."

"On another front, I stopped in to see Sloane's sister, Echo," Richard said. "She says she still hasn't heard from her brother."

"You think she's covering up for him?"

"No. I think she's worried about him. She did file that missing-person report right after he disappeared. I don't think she would have done that if she was trying to cover up his criminal activities. The neighbors said he was around her place a lot until he dropped off the face of the earth."

"There are a whole bunch of odd little angles to this case," Rand muttered.

Richard nodded. "Yeah, like why didn't Sid Edmonston report the break-in at Cranesbrook in the first place right after it happened?"

Before they could continue the conversation, a delivery person from the internal messenger service arrived and set a manila envelope on Rand's desk. He wasted no time opening it.

"Anything interesting?" Richard asked.

Rand shuffled through the papers. "The report on the hammer."

"And...?" Richard sat down and waited while Rand began reading the report. After finishing with the first sheet, he passed it over.

"So it's Tucker Hillman's blood on the hammer?" Richard said.

"Yeah. We have a positive identification on that. But no fingerprints."

"Which brings us back to the theory that someone else did it and wiped the hammer clean."

Richard nodded.

"You think Darnell is innocent?"

"Of murder. But we've still got to proceed as though he's the chief suspect."

"If he didn't do it, then who did?"

"Morton?" Rand asked.

"What's his motive?"

Rand shrugged. "I don't know. But maybe we

can get him to talk. Or Edmonston. Or one of the guys in his lab. Nelson Ulrich seems the most suspicious."

"Yeah. Of course, he could be working with Darnell. Or with Brayden Sloane. In fact, Sloane could be the ringleader in some kind of plot involving Cranesbrook."

They'd already discussed those possibilities. They were just rehashing old theories again.

"I'd like to make some progress," Rand muttered.

"Why don't we get Maxine Wallace to go back to Beech Grove and reinterview the staff?" Richard suggested.

"She's just a patrol officer."

"Yeah, but she seemed to be on the ball. And she might get some information we can't."

"What's your thinking on that?"

"Well, there's the small-town angle. She's local, and so is most of the staff at Beech Grove. They might open up with her more than with us. Then there's the female angle. You know, sometimes women will tell stuff to another woman that they won't say to a man."

Rand nodded. "It's all we've got."

GAGE FOUND another cheap motel outside Oxford, a town near St. Stephens, and got some sleep. He felt as though he'd been on the run for weeks, and he wasn't any closer to clearing his name than he had been when he'd busted out of Beech Grove. In fact, he was worse off. Now his picture was all over the television and the newspapers.

The photograph had been taken three years ago to go with the press release he and Bray had written when they'd first started Five Star Security. He was amazed at how young and confident he looked. He and Bray had been ready to take on the world then. Now he was a murder suspect and Bray was Lord knew where.

Until the explosion, he would have trusted Brayden Sloane with his life. Now he didn't know what to think. Had his partner made a secret deal with someone at Cranesbrook? Or a secret deal with someone who wanted to steal the results of the company's research? That was another possibility. Bray could even have been working with Evan Buckley, although they'd discussed the guy and Bray had concurred with Gage's assessment. That could just have been a tactic to throw Gage off the scent.

Gage ran his hand through his darkened hair. He was second-guessing everything that had happened over the past few weeks. It was just as likely that Bray was dead. He'd like to ask his sister, Echo, if she'd heard from him. But contacting her was simply too dangerous. Using a legal pad he'd bought, he wrote some lists of suspects and possibilities because seeing stuff in black and white always helped him think. Then he tore up the notes and flushed them down the toilet.

He tried to get some sleep on the lumpy motel mattress, but he tossed and turned most of the night. After checking out, he drove to a shopping mall in Rehoboth Beach, Delaware, where he bought camping equipment and some food. Then he headed back to Maryland, to an estate called Oak Lawn that was vacant ten months of the year. He'd camped there before, down by the Miles River, and he thought it was a good spot to hide out.

It had another advantage, too. It was only a few miles from Cranesbrook. Since the interviews he'd planned hadn't panned out, he needed to get back inside the company compound.

He wanted to look at the scene of the explosion and the lab records, specifically notes that wouldn't be available on computer. And he wanted to talk to Riddell.

Later, he could hack into the Cranesbrook system. But that would mean buying a computer and setting it up somewhere.

After pitching his tent, he laid out a security

perimeter around his campsite. If anyone tried to sneak up on him, he'd know about it before they got close enough to do any damage.

With a Sig tucked into the waistband of his shorts, he went for a run across the fields bordering the river. After being cooped up for days, it felt good to stretch his legs and work his muscles. And good to know that he was getting back into reasonable shape.

He stopped to wolf down a power bar, then practiced his climbing skills on a maple tree. After the exertion, he stripped off his clothes and quickly washed at one of the faucets scattered around the grounds that were used for watering the shrubbery. It was cold water but that was the best he was going to get out here.

Next he drove over to the Cranesbrook compound, just to have a look at the setup. Staying well out of range of the security cameras, he used binoculars to inspect the guard at the front gate. The man was wearing the uniform of Ace Security—the company that had bid against him for the original contract.

He'd expected that someone else would be handling the Cranesbrook detail. Still it made his throat tighten to see that his men were out of a job. Or maybe Peggy Olson had shuffled them into other assignments. He hoped so, but he couldn't ask her about it. That would get her involved and he'd already done enough damage to Lily by doing that.

Feeling somewhat deflated, he returned to camp. With the automatic weapon at his side, he cooked himself some Polish sausage and beans on the camp stove, and ate them along with some crudités from the refrigerator case at the grocery.

Crudités. He grinned. The first time he'd seen Lily write that word on a menu, he'd had no idea what it was.

She'd laughed and told him they were cut, raw vegetables.

His first lesson from his wife in fine dining.

Thinking of her made his heart squeeze. Was she all right? Were the cops hounding her? How did she feel about helping him escape?

He ached to call her and make sure she was doing okay. Knowing that could be a fatal mistake, he went back to the simple meal. He liked camp food and could live like this for a long time. But he wanted it to be *his* choice, not because he was running from the law.

He wanted his life back. His good name. His wife.

He closed his eyes, unable to keep himself from thinking about Lily again. At the Wilson estate, she could have run right outside and told the cops about his escape route, but she'd helped him get away. That meant she believed he wasn't a murderer. At least he hoped that was true.

He wanted to talk to her about it.

Talk?

What he really wanted was to feel her arms around him. Feel her lips on his. Feel her body warm and pliant in his arms.

The mere thought of making love to Lily turned him on. He had to stop that fantasy.

Until he cleared his name, he couldn't see her again. Not even if he staged another kidnapping. No more tricks like that.

He'd better focus on Cranesbrook and what he was going to do to help himself.

And first, he needed to check his powers. How much juice did he have, exactly?

He walked through the woods and picked up several pieces of wood that he might have used for a campfire, if he'd thought a campfire wasn't too dangerous under the current circumstances.

After setting a small log on the ground, he walked about ten feet away and tried to send his thoughts toward it.

He imagined it breaking in half. Though sweat broke out on his forehead, nothing happened.

Had he lost the talent?

That thought sent panic surging through him. Trotting up to the log, he took it in his hands and tried the experiment again. This time it snapped in half without him exerting any physical pressure, and he breathed out a small sigh.

It was amazing how quickly his panic had blossomed. A few days ago he hadn't possessed the ability to affect the physical world with his mind. Now he was starting to rely on it. That wasn't good. On the other hand, he wouldn't have been able to escape from Beech Grove or get away from the cops twice if he hadn't been able to work those tricks.

With a sense of fatalism, he set another log on the ground, then took a couple of steps back.

Once again he focused on snapping the wood with his thoughts. And once again he was able to do it.

He took five paces away from the next log. This time, every muscle in his body tensed as he struggled to break the wood.

Nothing happened. Five paces was too far, but four turned out to work. So he knew his range. And perhaps he could improve it with practice.

He spent the late afternoon resting. Before dark, he wiped down the pickup truck, making sure he hadn't left any fingerprints. Not that he expected anyone to impound the vehicle. But he wasn't taking any chances.

After dark, he smeared ashes on his face and donned a black shirt, slacks and shoes, along with a pair of thin leather gloves.

With the gun jammed into his waistband and a knapsack beside him on the passenger seat, he drove to the facility where he'd worked until last week.

If he got caught here, his ass was grass. So he had to avoid capture at all cost.

Erring on the side of caution, he kept well down the road as he watched the gatehouse through night-vision binoculars. After dark, there were two guards instead of one.

Slipping through the woods, he took up a position fifty yards from the front gate where the woods came close to the barrier. Then he leaned far enough out from behind a tree trunk to train his gaze on the walkway along the fence. When a guard came along, he noted the time, then waited for several cycles.

He'd had his men patrolling every twenty minutes. The present system was down to twelve minutes. Which meant he'd have to work fast to get inside.

He thought about how best to get into the compound. Because of the cement walkway, he couldn't dig his way under. And he couldn't go through. He'd been able to open, and reclose, the bars on the fence around Beech Grove, but this fence was wire mesh. If he opened a hole in it, he wasn't sure he could put it back together the way he'd found it.

He scanned the barrier again. It was festooned at the top with razor wire. Maybe he could make a break in a section of the wire then put them back together again when he came out.

That was the best plan he could think of. But it had its risks. Although the experiments with the logs had proved that he wouldn't have to climb the fence to work on the wire, he'd have to be standing right next to it to be effective.

As soon as the guard passed, he got down on his belly and slithered toward the fence, staying as low to the ground as he could. After he'd crossed the intervening space, he stood up beside the fence and focused on the razor wire.

It was four feet above his head. And working on it wasn't as easy as splitting a piece of wood under test conditions.

He'd been standing there for less than a minute when a spotlight switched on and swung toward him.

"There. Over by the woods," an excited voice shouted.

"Get him."

Gage jumped away from the fence and turning, dashed toward the woods. Once again, he heard the sound of gunshots, but he didn't spare the breath to curse.

He ran flat-out through the trees, making for the truck that he'd left on a turnoff along the two-lane road.

Footsteps pounded behind him. He knew that if he didn't get away, they were going to bring him down.

He reached the truck, leaped inside and started the engine. The wheels spun on gravel, but he managed to roar onto the road.

The bullets didn't stop. He heard one plow into the back left fender. Another hit the bumper, and he was glad he'd thought to disable the light over the license plate. Still, he was going to have to change vehicles again, since he couldn't drive around in something that looked like it had previously operated in Baghdad.

As he roared down the secondary road, headlights appeared behind him. He kept up his speed, then glanced at the instrument panel and saw that the gas gauge was dropping.

His angry curse filled the interior of the vehicle. They'd hit the gas tank.

So how long could he keep driving? Ten minutes? Less?

He made a sharp turn onto the highway and kept going, praying that he could get far enough to outrun the bastards in back of him.

Did they know it was him? Or were they under orders to cut down anyone who tried to get into the compound?

His nerves were jumping as he drove into the night, away from the estate where he'd left his stuff. He didn't want them to think he was staying anywhere in the vicinity.

Praying that he still had enough gas for another few minutes, he switched to a road that paralleled one of the many rivers snaking through the low-lying coastal region. When the engine started sputtering, he slowed and angled the vehicle toward the water.

Opening the door, he flung himself out, hitting the ground in a roll as the car plunged forward into the river.

He was scraped up, but that seemed to be the worst of it. At least he could run for cover at top speed. When two SUVs roared to a stop, he waited in the underbrush to find out what would happen next.

He could hear excited voices.

"Looks like he went into the water."

"The truck did. Maybe we'd better search the area."

Fading into the underbrush, he trotted away, staying parallel to the road but keeping under cover until he was a half mile from the scene where he'd ditched the truck.

When he came to a house with a couple of vehicles pulled up in the driveway, he made a quick decision. He was sick of stealing cars, but he didn't have much choice. Every minute that he stayed on foot increased the likelihood that the guards would spot him. So he picked the scruffiest car and unlocked the door. Then he rolled it down the driveway, using his muscles and his mind to move the car along. When he was about fifty yards from the house, he started the engine and drove away.

He left the car in Oxford and took another one that looked as though it belonged to people who had left the Eastern Shore for the winter season.

With his tracks pretty well covered, he headed back to his campsite. He'd thought he could get into Cranesbrook. That had obviously been a mistake.

LILY FINISHED UP her shift at the restaurant, then crossed the parking lot to the employee area. She couldn't shake the feeling that she was being followed. When she pulled out of her parking space, she saw a car at the other end of the lot switch on its lights.

It pulled out after her, and she speeded up. Once in traffic it seemed that she lost the tail, but she'd seen enough cop shows to know that you didn't have to see somebody behind you to have them following you. They could be using communications equipment and two or three cars. Or they could have put a tracking device on her car.

She was watchful as she pulled into her own driveway and saw an SUV glide past.

Were they tapping her phone, too? She was going to have to assume that was true.

After closing the blinds, she began selecting a few items of clothing and some toilet articles, all of which she packed into a plastic bag. The past few days she'd deliberately taken a large purse to work. Now she emptied out most of the contents and shoved the plastic bag inside.

In the morning, she choked down a little breakfast and called her sister.

"Pam?"

"Lily! How are you doing?"

"Not too bad, under the circumstances."

"It's got to be rough for you."

"Yes."

"You haven't heard anything about Gage?"

"No." She cleared her throat, hoping to get her sister's cooperation without giving anything away in case the cops were listening. "I know I'm not exactly the daughter Mom and Dad wanted."

"Don't say that! They love you."

"I hope so. Because at a time like this, you need your family. I wanted to go over and see them."

A year and a half ago, Barbara and Daryl Pindell had moved down to Maryland. Not to be near her, she was pretty sure. But so they could be close to Pam who had married an eye specialist from Johns Hopkins Hospital instead of a guy struggling to establish his own security business.

"But you know how they are," she continued. "Would you mind meeting me over there? That way, you know, you can sort of act as a buffer if they give me any grief."

Pam made a sound of commiseration. "Oh, Lily, I understand. Of course I'll meet you there."

"What time?"

"How about noon? They're always home then."

"Unless they're going out to lunch."

"This is Tuesday," Lily reminded her. "Not a lunch day."

"Oh, right. How could I forget?"

They both laughed.

"Thanks," Lily said. She hung up, wondering if her plan was going to work, since she hadn't been able to explain anything to her sister.

She spent a restless morning. At eleven-thirty, she got dressed in cropped pants and a top and tied a bright scarf around her head.

As she drove to her parent's new house off upper Charles Street in Baltimore, she spotted a car following her. This time she was making the tail a part of her plans.

Pam was already at the house, and Lily parked her Toyota behind her sister's Mercedes.

Mildred, her parents' longtime maid who had come from Philadelphia with them, greeted her at the front door.

"Miss Lily, how are you?" she asked sympathetically.

"As well as can be expected. Are my parents in the sunroom?" she asked. Stupid question. They'd found a mansion as much as possible like their old one, and they kept to the same routine.

Mildred stepped aside, and Lily walked to the back of the house. Her parents were already sitting at a glass-topped table under a huge ficus tree. Mom wore a flowered dress, and Dad had on a sports coat, as if they were expecting company, not their daughters. But they'd always been formal people. Pam was standing at one of the large windows, looking out at the garden.

She turned and crossed the room, and they embraced.

"Thank you for coming," Lily murmured.

"Is there anything I can do for you?"

"We can talk about that later."

Their mother interrupted the exchange, addressing Lily. "Pam told us you were coming. You could have phoned ahead."

"Sorry," Lily apologized, thinking that nothing had changed. Some people mellowed as they aged. Apparently her mother wasn't one of them.

"They've stopped running your husband's picture in the paper every day," her father said. "That's good."

"It's so embarrassing to have our friends calling and asking questions," Barbara murmured.

"Sorry," Lily said again. Over the tops of Daryl and Barbara's heads, she and her sister exchanged a knowing look.

The Pindells had been very conscious of their place in Philadelphia society. And when they'd come to Baltimore, they'd joined one of the most expensive and prestigious country clubs to establish their credentials in the new environment.

Daryl Pindell's family had made its money long ago in the shipping business, then diversified into various industries. In retirement, he and his wife kept busy playing golf and bridge and attending various charity events in Baltimore and in Philadelphia.

It was a lifestyle that made both Pam and Lily cringe. Neither one of them had ever considered a life of leisure.

Pam worked as a receptionist in her husband's office several days a week. Lily had completely broken with family tradition when she'd announced she wanted to go to culinary school. Then she'd had the bad judgment to marry a man from the wrong side of the tracks. And recently, he'd proved how egregious a choice he really was.

After joining her parents at the table, Lily said, "Things are going pretty well at the restaurant."

"You should have your own place by now," her father said.

"Well, I'm getting recognition for my work," she offered. "*Baltimore Magazine* did a piece on me in the spring."

They were silent for several moments. Then she cleared her throat. "With Gage out of town, things are kind of tight. I was wondering if I could borrow a little money from you."

"Out of town! That's a good way to put it," Barbara commented.

Lily clasped her hands in front of her on the table.

"How much do you want to borrow?" her father asked.

"A thousand dollars would be a big help."

"You've never taken money from us in the past," her mother observed.

"Gage wanted to make it on his own," Lily answered, then wondered if anyone would make a snide comment.

Mercifully, her mother kept silent and her father said, "We'd be glad to help you out now."

Lily gave him a grateful look. She'd always wondered what he would have been like if he'd married a different woman. But he'd gone along with his parents' plans to hook him up with the right sort of bride.

"Pam says you're staying to lunch," Barbara said.

"Yes. Thanks."

Mildred served chicken salad and fruit. Lily knew it had to be excellent, but it tasted like straw in her mouth. Still, she managed to eat a little and not to protest when her mother gave her the standard lecture on Gage Darnell. Well, not the standard lecture, since Gage had certainly outdone himself now.

Dad excused himself and came back with the money he'd promised, and she thanked him sincerely.

Then she stood and looked at her sister. "I need to talk to you about something."

"Okay."

They walked down the hall and stepped into the den.

"I'm sorry you had to listen to all that," Pam murmured.

"I'm used to it. It just rolls off my back." She gave her sister a direct look. "I need a big favor. The police are following me. I want to get out of here without their knowing."

"How can you do that?"

"I was thinking that if you change clothes and cars with me, they'll follow the wrong sister."

Pam grinned. "Clever. I was wondering why you wore a scarf on your head."

"You'll do it?"

"Of course. Where are you going?"

"It's better if I don't tell you."

"Right."

"We should say goodbye to Mom and Dad now. If they don't see us leave, they can't tell anyone later about our clothing exchange."

Pam nodded. After thanking their parents for

lunch, they went back to the powder room and swapped clothes.

Pam was now wearing Lily's cropped pants and top, while Lily had on Pam's sundress. Since they were both the same size, the clothing fit perfectly.

When Pam refolded Lily's scarf into a triangle and tied it under her chin, a wisp of blond hair peeked out, but that was good because it was similar to Lily's.

They switched sunglasses and swapped car keys. Pam took the big purse, minus the plastic bag of clothing.

"You go first," Lily said. "Then whoever is lurking out there will follow you." She dragged in a breath and let it out. "Sorry about your car. I'm not sure when I can get it back to you."

"Don't worry about it." Pam thought for a moment. "I guess I shouldn't go right home or the cops will wonder why you're driving up to my house."

"Do you need an excuse to go shopping?"

Pam grinned. "No. I'll go to the mall and hit the women's clothing sales. That should stupefy any guy assigned to follow me."

"Yeah, take him on a trip through the bra section."

They laughed together. Then Lily sobered. "Oh,

Pam, thank you," she breathed, fighting not to choke up as her vision clouded.

After they embraced, Pam walked out the front door and climbed into Lily's Toyota.

Lily watched through the window. Down the street, a car slipped away from the curb. Presumably her tail.

She'd find out soon enough if she'd fooled the cops.

Chapter Ten

Lily Darnell had given her tail the slip. That trick with the sister had been pretty clever. Rand had to give her that.

And he had another case of tricky maneuvers to investigate as well.

Maxine Wallace had called with some startling news. In her interviews at Beech Grove, the officer had discovered that a Cranesbrook employee named Hank Riddell had been at the hospital keeping tabs on Gage Darnell and Wes Vanderhoven.

What the hell was that all about?

Rand and Richard did a little research on the man and found he was a recent PhD from Cornell University who had joined the staff nine months ago. He was unmarried and living in a rented house about twenty minutes from the facility.

When they called Cranesbrook, they were told he

wasn't on site. At his house, they found out from a neighbor that he'd been living at the research facility since Darnell's escape from the hospital.

"Son of a bitch," Richard muttered. "Either the right hand doesn't know what the left hand is doing or somebody out there is deliberately sending out false information."

"Let's see what the president of the company says."

They drove back to the campus. In Sid Edmonston's office, Rand kept his gaze fixed on the man as he said, "We have some questions about Hank Riddell's role at Beech Grove. Apparently he was sent out there for some purpose after two of your employees were admitted as patients."

"He was dispatched there to protect our interests."

"How exactly?"

"We wanted to be kept informed of Darnell's and Vanderhoven's conditions."

"You could have gotten the information in a phone call," Richard pointed out.

"As you might have noticed, Dr. Morton isn't very forthcoming with reports on patients."

"Vanderhoven's still at Beech Grove. Why isn't Riddell still there?"

"Vanderhoven's status hasn't changed, so we decided to call back our valued employee."

Rand listened to Edmonston's convoluted speech. The man was obviously nervous about answering these questions. "So why did you send a PhD scientist to do the job?" Rand pressed.

"He was available and he's a personal friend of Wes Vanderhoven's. Riddell was worried about him, so we let him do the work."

"Why did the switchboard say he wasn't here when we called this morning?"

"He's been working the night shift. He was sleeping in one of our dorms, and he'd left instructions not to be disturbed. Apparently he simply chose to say he wasn't here."

"Well, we'd like to talk to him," Rand said.

Edmonston hesitated. Then he must have decided that the best policy was to give in gracefully. He picked up the phone and called the dorm. When he got off the phone he looked up. "He's up. You can go over there now."

They got directions and left the executive offices.

"You think Edmonston is talking to Riddell on the phone right now?" Rand asked.

"Yeah, I do," Richard agreed. "So let's get over there before they cook up a story together."

Quickly they strode into a building that looked like an upscale motel. When they arrived, Riddell, a sandy-haired young man of medium height, was in the small cafeteria, pouring himself a cup of coffee. He straightened his spine and rose up on his toes when they came in. They both noted that he was standing eight feet from a wall phone.

"We appreciate your talking to us," Rand said.

"Not a problem." The scientist took his coffee mug to a small table and sat down.

Rand and Richard also sat.

"You've been here for the past week and a half?" Rand asked.

"I've had a lot of work to do. It was easier to stay on campus, particularly now that we've got security problems."

Richard pulled out his notebook and wrote it down.

"You were at Beech Grove keeping tabs on Darnell and Vanderhoven?"

"Yes. Project Cypress is an important project."

"Project Cypress?"

Riddell looked flustered. "Yes, that's where we had the lab accident."

"What's the purpose of the project?"

"I'm afraid I can't tell you that. It's proprietary information."

"Okay," Rand agreed, since he knew they wouldn't get anywhere digging into that.

"Who sent you to Beech Grove?" Richard asked.

"Dr. Ulrich."

"Why?" Rand asked, keeping up the flow of questions.

Riddell took a sip of coffee. "Wes and I are friends. I wanted to keep tabs on how he was doing."

"But Vanderhoven is still in the hospital. Why did you come back to the lab?"

"Wes's condition hasn't changed. I wasn't accomplishing anything by hanging around there and I needed to get back to work."

He was giving the same answers as Edmonston, which probably meant that they'd just synchronized their stories.

"You had a specific assignment at the hospital?"

"We wanted to monitor any damaging effects from the lab accident."

"Were there any damaging effects?" Richard pressed.

"Both men were initially violent. It looks like Darnell stayed that way. So they've kept Wes under sedation."

"What's his prognosis?"

"There's no use asking me medical questions."

"But you were sent over there to make medical observations," Rand said.

Riddell sighed. "I was sent to observe."

It was obvious this guy was hiding something—and they weren't going to get it out of him at this interview.

"Thanks for your time," Rand said before they went back to have another try at Sid Edmonston.

"Did you get what you needed from Hank Riddell?" he asked pleasantly when they were back in his office.

"He's pretty closed up."

"He's an introverted scientist type," Edmonston shot back. "And he's worried about his friend."

Rand switched tactics. "Are the experiments in your lab back on track?"

"Yes," the company president answered.

"Since the incident, have any of your employees given you reason to be suspicious of them?"

"A lab assistant and one of the women on our administrative staff quit abruptly. But they could just be nervous about the fallout from the explosion."

"I'd like their names," Rand said.

Edmonston wrote them down and handed the paper across the desk.

"What about security? Any more problems?"

The executive's gaze shifted away. "Security is fine," he said.

Rand thought he detected a lie, and he wanted

to probe that answer. But Edmonston switched the subject abruptly.

"I keep wondering if Darnell is hanging around the area."

"Why?"

"He left a lot of valuable equipment in the security office when he cleared out."

"If he's still around, where do you think he would be?"

Edmonston was silent for several moments.

Finally, he cleared his throat and said, "I've talked to a lot of people on the staff about him. I've learned he went camping out. That would avoid contact with motel owners, wouldn't it?"

"Where did he camp?"

"I heard he liked the state park. And an estate along the river."

"Named?"

"Oak Lawn."

Since Edmonston didn't have any other suggestions, they left several minutes later.

"If he's around here, do you think the wife is with him?" Richard asked.

"She went to a lot of trouble to give us the slip. I don't think she just wanted to get away to a beauty spa. And she was willing to risk getting fired, since she hasn't shown up to work."

Rand switched back to the interview with the company president. "What about Edmonston? You think he was telling the truth?"

"He's lying about something."

"So is Riddell. But what?"

"I don't know. Maybe it's got to do with the work the lab is doing. Maybe he and Riddell are working something dirty and they don't want us to know about it, so they switched the focus to Darnell. I'd like to know what Project Cypress is exactly. Riddell was upset that he'd blurted out the name."

"Yeah."

"Back to Edmonston. Maybe he wants us to take down Darnell but he doesn't want us to know it."

"What would be the point of that?"

"Maybe he knows Darnell could give us some embarrassing information about Project Cypress."

"Which brings us back to the theory that Darnell is innocent," Rand mused. "I'd give a lot to ask him some questions about what happened the night of the explosion and then later in the hospital, since we haven't gotten anything but psychobabble from Dr. Morton."

Richard nodded.

Often, their conversations ran along the same track. They were the perfect working team—and also good friends. Rand wasn't married, so he spent a lot of holidays at Richard's house with his wife and two kids.

"Even if Darnell is innocent, he's made it clear that he's determined not to get caught. We can't take a chance on his trying to shoot his way out of an ambush."

"Which means we'd better approach him with extreme caution."

IT WAS ten in the evening. Gage had fixed another great camp meal—ground beef and flavored rice. After cleaning up, he sat down on a log where he could indulge in a chocolate bar and stare at the river while he contemplated his next move.

He was watching the lights of a speedboat go by when the vibration of the alarm system intruded on his evening.

Son of a bitch. They'd found him.

He left the camp lantern on as a decoy, then quickly reached in his pack for his night-vision goggles. The Sig was already in his waistband.

He was never without it now. It even sat within reach when he was washing off at the water faucet.

The alarm was sophisticated. He could have checked on the GPS screen in the tent but the kind of vibration told him from which direction the intruder had come.

Putting on the goggles, he looked away from the light and toward the house, where he saw someone slip through the woods, moving stealthily from tree to tree. They seemed to be heading for the tent, and he'd guess that they hadn't figured out he wasn't inside.

Big mistake. As far as Gage could see, the guy was on the small side, and dressed in a black T-shirt and dark jeans. Details were obscured by the trees and by the baseball cap that partially hid the intruder's face.

Maybe it wasn't the cops. Maybe it was someone figuring to be a hero by capturing the unauthorized person camping on the estate.

While Mr. Stealth snuck up on the tent, Gage got into position behind him.

In the Special Forces he'd learned to glide through the natural environment with almost no noise. He was able to get directly behind the guy. Then, with a sudden rush of movement, he leaped from the bushes, grabbed the man around the neck and brought him down.

Mr. Stealth made a gurgling sound as he hit the ground. Gage came down on top of him, losing his goggles in the process. But he didn't need them to see what he was doing as he rolled the invader to his back and straddled him, clamping the guy's arms to his sides.

The man lay still for a second, then heaved up, trying to dislodge Gage's knees, which were on either side of his body.

"Shut up and don't move, or I'll blow your head off," Gage growled as he shoved the Sig against the guy's temple.

The fellow stilled, except for the shiver that went through his body.

Holding the gun steady, Gage reached to pull off the baseball cap.

As they stared at each other, they both gasped.

"Lily! What the hell are you doing here?" The shock of seeing her was like an electric current coursing through his body.

"Hoping I'd find you," she said in a voice that he knew she was struggling to hold steady.

He glanced around. "And leading the cops right to me?"

"No. I'm not that dumb. I worked out how to do it. I met my sister at my parents' house and asked if she'd help me."

"Your parents! I'll bet they loved that."

"They have no idea what I planned.' Lily told him about the clothing switch.

"When she left, I watched the cops follow her. After I got into her car and drove away, I spent a lot of time making sure nobody was tailing me."

"They could have been using two or three cars. Or a transponder."

"I know that. I said, we traded cars. So if they put a transponder on my car, they'd still end up following her."

"Okay," he said slowly, suddenly aware that he was still sitting on top of Lily.

"Gage?" she whispered. "How about putting down your gun?"

"Not yet." He hadn't escaped capture for this long by being careless.

He stood up, then reached with his free hand to help Lily to her feet.

As soon as she was standing, he put the goggles back on and carefully surveyed the surrounding area, then motioned her to follow him through the woods.

He knew he was using the time to collect his scattered thoughts. When the glow of the lantern in the tent hurt his eyes, he took off the goggles.

"How did you find me?" he asked in a voice that sounded gruff to his own ears.

"We came here together once. I thought it might be a good place for you to hide out."

"Yeah."

"I figured you'd stay in the area, and stay under cover." She tipped her head to the side, trying to get a look at him in the darkness. "And I knew you'd change your appearance. I tried the camp-ground at the state park first. When you weren't there, I came here."

"Why did you think I'd hang around? It would make more sense for me to run away."

"Because you want to clear your name," she answered, conviction ringing in her voice.

"And now you're confident that I didn't murder anyone?"

"Yes." Her breath hitched. "I guess I can't convince you I believe you by kissing you."

"Unfortunately, you tried that trick before."

"Last time it was a trick. This time it's not." She made a low sound and closed the space between them, clasping her arms around him and holding him tight.

If he knew what was good for him, he would pull away, but the feel of her arms made it impos-sible for him to move.

Warnings flickered in his brain. Last time he had convinced himself that she was feeling the same needs as he. And he'd let wishful thinking fuel his arousal. This could be an elaborate scam, and the cops could be waiting in the woods for him to drop his defenses.

But he wasn't exhausted and confused like he'd been the night he'd escaped from Beech Grove. Tonight he was pretty sure he could figure out the difference between glass and diamonds.

Before she could speak, he brought his lips down on hers and felt a jolt of hot sensation arch between them.

It was like being hit by a bolt of lightning. He wavered on his feet, then moved backward, dragging her with him as he braced his hips against the trunk of a tree—all without breaking the mouth-to-mouth contact.

His tongue probed the hot interior of her mouth, and she made a sound that tasted of surrender.

Yet he still couldn't entirely relax. Even if she hadn't brought the cops, he half expected her to be afraid of a man who had shown her what he could do with his mind.

She should be afraid. She should run in the other direction. Instead, she had come looking for him. And now she was kissing him with all the passion he remembered so well.

She slumped against him, and he tightened his grip on her, holding the two of them up.

"Gage, I missed you so much," she whispered,

her fingers brushing the bristly hairs of the beard he was growing.

He opened his eyes, surprised at the darkness of the night. He felt so hot that he half expected the air around them to glow.

The rational part of his mind told him he should send her away—for a dozen different reasons. But he had lost the ability to turn her loose. She was too warm and willing in his arms, and he knew that if he didn't make love with her, he would go insane.

She brought her mouth back to his, sending heat blazing through him as she moved in closer, increasing the intimacy of their contact.

At the same time, her lips stroked over his, coaxing, exploring, inciting.

"Let me show you how much I need you," she whispered into his mouth.

As he drank in the words and the taste of her—new and yet familiar—he felt the pounding of his own heart against her breasts.

When she moved against his erection, he thought he would go up in flames.

He was within moments of tearing off her pants, lowering his zipper and lifting her into his arms so he could plunge into her. But then their joining would be over much too fast.

Perhaps she was following the same line of

thinking, because her voice reached his ears as a heady whisper.

"I want to feel you on top of me."

Knitting his fingers with hers, he led her through the darkness to the lantern glow of the tent.

He was no longer thinking about the cops following her here. There was so little blood in his brain that he was capable of only one thought—taking the suggestion she'd just made.

Bending, she crawled inside the tent, kicking off her shoes as she went.

He did the same, only he stopped to pull off his shirt before he got inside. When he was free of the obstruction, he saw that she had discarded her bra along with her shirt.

In the warm glow from the lantern, she smiled at him. He stowed the gun along the side of the tent, then eased onto the sleeping bag beside Lily, feeling as though he had finally come home after a long journey.

His hands were drawn to her beautiful breasts. Tenderly, he cradled the soft mounds in his hands, stroking his thumbs across the tightened nipples.

She sighed and held out her arms, and he came into her embrace, feeling her breasts against his chest.

Leaning back, he pulled her on top of him, adjusting her position until the hard shaft of his erection nestled in the cleft at the top of her legs.

Heat surged between them. And emotions so raw and honest that he cried out in wonder.

"Yes," she whispered.

His arms came around her, holding her to him, his ragged breathing mingling with hers.

"I want you naked. And inside me."

"Yes." As he spoke, his hands stroked the silky skin of her back, pressing her breasts against his chest.

By mutual agreement, they broke apart and each tore at the remainder of their own clothing.

Then they came back together, lying on their sides, clasping each other tightly and rocking back and forth on the blanket.

"Now. Please, now," she breathed.

She rolled to her back and reached for his erection, guiding him to her. As he covered her body with his and plunged into her tight heat, she cried out in pleasure.

Sexual need leaped between them. And at the same time, he felt as though a healing balm had washed over him.

"Thank you for trusting me," he whispered.

"Thank you for forgiving me," she answered.

He clasped the back of her head, bringing his

mouth back to her, kissing her with lips and teeth and tongue as he moved in a steady rhythm, plunging into her and withdrawing.

They each made a greedy sound as their need for release spiraled out of control. When he felt her come undone, he followed her over the edge, crying out with the intensity of his climax.

Collapsing on top of her, he lay panting.

Her hands stroked over his damp shoulders, then his hair.

When he rolled to his side, he kept her with him.

"I am so sorry about what I did at the Wilson estate."

"I understand. I should have told you what was going on with me, but I thought I'd just be giving you another reason to think I was crazy."

"Your demonstration was pretty convincing."

"It took me awhile to think of it."

"I guess you're not used to working magic."

"Not magic."

"Then what?"

"Paranormal ability."

"Whatever."

Keeping his voice even, he asked, "You're not worried about it?"

She hitched in a breath and let it out. "Maybe a little."

He appreciated the honesty of the answer. Closing his eyes, he nibbled his lips against her cheek, then down to the tender place just below her jaw.

"I let myself forget how good this was," he murmured. "Not just the sex. The part afterward when I get to hold you in my arms and cuddle you."

She sounded dreamy as she answered, "I missed you. So much."

"Me, too. And not just the past few days. Lily, I'm the one who should be apologizing—for forgetting about what's important in our lives. I was too focused on chasing success. Maybe I was really trying to be the kind of guy your parents would be glad you married. And look where it got me."

"Don't!"

"I have to explain."

She pressed her fingers to his lips. "Let's not spoil the cuddling."

"Sorry." He managed to keep silent for several moments. But now that they'd made love, he couldn't stop his mind from racing. "If you stay with me, you're on the run from the cops, too."

"At the moment I'm too tired for a deep discussion. We can talk in the morning."

"We have to be realistic. Maybe the best thing is for you to go back home. If you do that, they won't know you were even down here."

"How do I explain the part about switching clothes and cars with Pam?"

"You can say you were just tired of being followed. And you wanted to make a point."

"I could. But I'm staying with you," she said, and he heard the determination in her voice.

"It's not very comfortable here. You're sure you want to live in a tent?"

"If you're here with me."

He felt his throat close. He'd been a fool to neglect this woman, but there were things they had to talk about.

"What about your job?"

"I…didn't show up for work. I'm sure I've been fired by now."

"No!"

"I'm good at what I do. I can get another job."

She'd burned her bridges. But still he had to point out the new reality. "If you stick with me, you're an accessory after the fact."

"Rand McClellan already told me that."

"He's one of those cops who came to our house and to the Wilson estate?"

She nodded. "Maryland State Police. After you escaped, he threatened to haul me in."

Gage made a rough sound. "My fault."

"Stop blaming yourself. You were desperate."

"Don't make excuses for me." He raised up and looked down into her eyes. "Why did he let you go?"

"First, he couldn't prove I'd done anything wrong. Then, I guess he figured I was more use to him on the loose."

He sat up and ran a shaky hand through his hair. "I've made a mess out of your life."

Her eyes turned fierce. "It's not exactly your fault. We're going to figure this out together."

Before he could object, she rushed on. "If something had happened to me, you'd do the same."

"Yeah," he answered in a low voice. "But there are factors you don't know about."

He felt her tense. "Like what?"

"I saw Hank Riddell, one of the guys who worked in Lab 7, at Beech Grove. He could be the guy who shot at me. Then there's Evan Buckley, one of my security men. I thought he might have been in on whatever went down at Cranesbrook. Now he's dead. Killed in a hit-and-run motorcycle accident—before I could question him. I have to assume that was murder."

She swallowed hard. "I'm sorry."

"At least they can't pin that murder on me. Or I don't *think* they can. It depends on how creative those detectives get."

"I think they're just trying to do their job," she murmured.

"You're right. Too bad we can't compare notes. We could probably help each other out. Like, I wonder if they've got a line on Bray."

"Where is he?"

"I wish I knew. Half the time I'm worried sick about him. And the other half, I wonder if he's in on it. What if he planned the explosion then ran out on me?"

She sat up and gave him a questioning look. "Why would he do that?"

He heaved out a sigh. "For money."

"But…"

"He was in serious debt."

"How? He's not married, and I thought he was pretty frugal. Did he gamble or something I don't know about?"

Gage shifted uncomfortably. "Nothing bad. I told you he was helping out his sister, Echo. I just didn't tell you how much it was costing."

Lily nodded. They hadn't discussed the Sloane family situation much, but they both knew that Echo Sloane had been pregnant and unmarried. She'd been too proud to turn to her brother for help when her boyfriend ran out on her. But Bray had stepped in and paid her hospital bills then helped support her and the baby.

"How much are we talking about?" Lily asked.

"She had some complications. Her hospital bills came to around fifty thousand dollars."

She whistled. "I didn't know."

"Bray didn't talk about it much, probably because we weren't making enough money to cover that kind of expense. What if he figured he had to do something illegal to pay those kind of debts? What if he'd borrowed from the mob, and they came after him for the money?"

"You and Bray were always there for each other. You really think he'd leave you twisting in the wind?"

"I wouldn't have bet on it." Gage tightened his fists, then deliberately released the pressure. "Now I don't know what the hell to think. If I could talk to him, maybe we could clear it all up. But he's disappeared." He kept the rest of it—his fear that Bray might be dead—to himself. But he knew Lily had taken in his darkening mood.

"We can't solve those problems now," she whispered.

To stop the discussion, she reached over and closed her hand around him. They'd made love less than an hour ago, but he found himself instantly responding. And when he looked over, he caught the smug expression on her face.

"You're not playing fair," he said in a thick voice as he dragged her close and brought his mouth down on hers, wondering how he had gotten along without her for so damn long.

She sighed his name. "I'm so glad you're back."

He was no prize, but he couldn't turn away from what she was offering.

JUST AFTER DAWN a low vibration woke Gage. The alarm had sounded again.

Only this time he knew it wasn't Lily sneaking up on him because she was sleeping beside him.

He heard someone approaching from down the road. But when he dug out the GPS screen, he saw other blips.

"Wake up."

She blinked and looked up at him. "What?"

"The honeymoon's over," he said in a gritty voice. "We've got company."

Chapter Eleven

While his wife pulled on her clothes—she didn't waste time with her bra—Gage squinted at the screen. "We've got six visitors."

Her eyes grew big. "Oh Lord, this has to be my fault."

"You don't know that! But however they found me, we have to get lost." He reconsidered. "Well, I have to. You could turn yourself in."

"You honestly think they'd believe I was innocent a second time?"

"No." He looked down at the screen. Two of the blips were moving slowly toward the tent. The other four remained stationary.

"They're moving cautiously, but they don't realize I know they're here and how many they are."

"How do we get away?" she asked.

He scrabbled together a plan. "You go first, while they're still getting into position. Keep low and head for the river, toward the marshy patch upstream where it'll be hard to see you go into the water. When you're clear of the area, swim downstream along the bank to the next estate. I hid a car in the woods down there and some supplies, in case I needed to leave here fast."

"What about you?"

"I've got a couple of things to do. Then I'll be right after you."

DETERMINED not to surrender to panic, Lily gave Gage a quick, hard kiss, then slipped out of the tent into another world. Thick, disorienting fog lay over the ground, obscuring the details of the landscape. It was difficult for her to figure out which way to go, but the cops had the same handicap.

Out in the fog, she felt as though icy fingers were dancing over her bare arms and neck. If she thought too much, she would go to pieces, so she kept her mind on the task Gage had given her. All she had to do was get to the river. Slip in without being seen. Then swim downstream to the next estate. Yeah, right.

The foggy air turned the campground into the set for a horror movie. The woods seemed empty. Not even a bird sang, but she knew the reason for that. The animals had spied the men sneaking

through the trees, and they'd taken off to somewhere safer.

Staying low, Lily surveyed the landscape, then
crept toward a break in the trees. As she drew
closer, she thought she could see blue-gray water
visible beyond the foliage.

She tried to keep her focus on getting away,
but guilt racked her. This had to be her fault. If
she hadn't gone looking for Gage, he'd still be
safe. Now she had to keep from blowing his
escape plan.

As she broke through the trees, she spotted a
line of large rocks probably put there to stabilize the shoreline. Unfortunately, she'd have to
climb over them to reach the water. She was just
getting ready to make a dash for the nearest rock
when the sound of a helicopter stopped her in
her tracks.

She craned her neck up and saw a shaft of light
coming down through the mist.

Gage had thought the river would be clear. But
the cops had covered that exit, too. How much
could the guys up there see? Did she have a
chance of making it into the water?

She watched thankfully as the helicopter moved
on. As soon as she was in the clear, Lily rushed
from cover and scrambled over the rocks. On the

other side, mud pulled at her shoes. She kicked them off, then carried them along with her, moving as fast as she could.

Her clothes were going to get in the way when she tried to swim. But leaving them on the bank would be too big a clue about where she'd gone.

Tucking the shoes under her arm, she kept running, unzipping her pants as she sloshed through the rushes.

At the water's edge, she thrust the shoes into the pants, then zipped them up again, using the pant legs to tie the whole thing into a ball.

Still wearing her T-shirt and panties, she started awkwardly swimming, dragging the clothing along with her until she was far enough out for them to sink.

GAGE BUNDLED his electronics equipment into a knapsack, thinking he'd rather lose it in the river than let the authorities find out about the advanced technology he was using. While he worked, he braced for the worst.

At the Wilson estate, the cops had called out to him with a bullhorn. This time the woods were silent.

Maybe he could get away. But what about Lily? He'd sucked her into this mess by letting her stay the night. Now he could only pray that she got to the river and off the property.

But she wasn't trained for this. And even if she made it off the estate, she didn't know where he'd hidden the car.

In this situation, he didn't see what good his new talent could do him. Better to rely on the tried and true—his Sig.

He grabbed the waterproof case with the electronics and thrust it into a net bag for easy carrying.

Outside the tent, he stayed low and held the small control panel in his hand, figuring he'd keep track of the enemy until the unit got too wet to function. From a quick glance at the screen, he saw that he didn't have much time before the cops had him boxed in.

He knew they were using a helicopter. He'd already heard it. Before he'd taken ten steps from the tent, it came sweeping back. In the next moment, a spotlight cut through the mist above him, missing him by a couple of feet.

Cursing under his breath, he hit the ground, waiting until the chopper began searching another part of the woods.

When the helicopter had made its first pass over the area, he started moving again, knowing the machine was going to come sweeping back.

Suddenly another sound stopped him. An exchange of gunfire behind him.

He leaped to the shelter of a tree trunk, pressing against the rough bark.

WHEN LILY was thirty feet from where she'd gone into the water, the unmistakable of sound of gunfire rang out through the early-morning air.

She froze in mid-stroke.

Gage! They were shooting at Gage. That was the only explanation that made sense. With her heart in her throat, she looked behind her. But the mist obscured the shoreline and the woods beyond.

Treading water, she remained in place, hoping against hope that she'd see Gage come scrambling over the rocks and take the same route she had into the river.

It didn't happen. From above, she heard a roaring noise. The helicopter was coming back. When it zoomed out of the fog, she dove below the surface, the water muffling the roar of the blades.

Still, it sounded as if the chopper was hanging directly over her.

She had taken a gulp of air before going down, but after half a minute, the oxygen began to solidify in her chest.

When she felt like her lungs were going to

burst, she knew she had to come up. But she held off for agonizing seconds longer, and to her vast relief, the sound of the blades receded into the background.

Kicking to the surface again, she gulped in air, shook the wet hair out of her eyes and looked around. The mist still hung low over the water, and she saw no one.

She should do what Gage had told her to do— get to the next estate, but now she felt too dispirited to swim. Gage had sent her on ahead and gotten caught by the cops.

When she saw movement along the shore, she ducked low, keeping only her nose and eyes above the water. From her covert position, she saw a figure climbing the rocks.

Her heart stopped, then started up again in double time as she saw Gage running through the marsh and into the water.

He stopped and thrust something into a net bag, then slung it over his shoulder again.

She wanted to shout his name, but she kept her lips pressed together. Treading water, she waited with her pulse pounding as he came closer to her.

She knew the exact moment when he spotted her. His eyes turned fierce. "Go!" he mouthed as he stripped off his pants and shoes.

She started swimming again, and he caught up before she'd gotten twenty yards farther.

"What are you doing here?" he demanded, keeping his voice low.

She ached to pull him into her arms and hang on. She had to content herself with moving close and pressing her shoulder to his. "I—I heard the gunfire," she gasped. "Are you all right? What happened?"

"I'm okay, but I don't know what happened. It sounded like they were shooting at each other."

She stared at him, trying to wrap her mind around that concept. "Why?"

"Maybe they got confused in the fog."

Before she could ask another question, he spoke again. "Move it before the chopper comes back."

She knew he was right, and she started stroking again. But she had never been a strong swimmer, and she felt as though she had been in the water for hours. As she struggled to follow Gage, her arms and legs began to feel like lead.

Even dragging a heavy case through the water, Gage plowed ahead—until he realized she wasn't beside him.

Dropping back, he asked, "Are you all right?"

"You go ahead."

"Don't be crazy!" He stayed beside her, jeopardizing his own safety.

Breathing hard, she kept swimming, glad that he was with her because she didn't know where they were going.

"This way."

With a feeling of relief, she stroked toward the shore, expelling a grateful sigh when her feet finally touched solid ground.

They'd entered the water through a marsh. Downriver, the beach was sandy. A lot better than the previous muck.

As she staggered out of the water, she looked over at Gage. He was wearing only a pair of swimming trunks, and she had on the proverbial wet T-shirt.

Gasping from the swim, she wanted to flop down on the sand and close her eyes. But Gage took hold of her arm.

"Sorry. We can't stay out in the open. If that chopper comes back and sees us, we're toast."

THE NOISE of the helicopter was like a buzz sounding in Rand's brain as he crouched over his partner, pressing his hand against the wadded-up jacket that wasn't doing much to stop the bleeding from Richard's chest.

One minute they'd both been sneaking up on

the campsite. Then shots had stopped them in their tracks.

Rand had ducked behind a tree, while Richard had returned fire. And he'd gotten hit.

"Hang on. Just hang on. The paramedics are coming," Rand whispered, still trying to stanch the blood seeping through his partner's shirt.

From where he lay in a pile of leaves, Richard looked up, the light fading from his eyes. When his eyelids flickered, Rand closed the fingers of his free hand around his partner's shoulder.

He could see Richard trying to focus on him.

"Stay awake," he ordered. "I know you want to go to sleep, but don't do it."

Richard's lips moved, but no words came out.

Time dragged by, and Rand cursed under his breath. Where were the damn paramedics?

In the next moment, he knew it was too late.

Still, Rand pressed two fingers to his partner's carotid artery. He felt nothing. Reaching up, he closed Richard's eyes, trying to wrap his mind around the realization that his partner was dead.

How had it happened? Nobody had acted like a damn hot dog. They'd cased the estate. They'd determined that someone was there—most likely Darnell. And they'd moved in slowly and carefully with a trained team.

Then, suddenly, it had all gone wrong. Darnell must have caught on to the attack and left the tent. Then he'd slipped into the woods. Instead of clearing out of the area, he'd circled around them and started shooting.

Rand had escaped the trap. But Richard was dead.

He still couldn't believe it. The attack had been too fast and too unexpected.

"Bastard," he muttered. He didn't know whether he was talking to himself or Richard. "He won't get away. I swear it. I'll track him down and bring him in—dead or alive. Preferably dead."

It seemed incredible that he'd felt sorry for Gage Darnell. He'd started to think that the guy might have been set up. Obviously that had been a bunch of crap. First Darnell had killed the janitor when the man had gotten in his way. Then he'd turned and fired on the police when he could have run. That meant he was spiraling out of control.

"I'll get him," he repeated, this time knowing he was making the promise to Richard. The vow made him feel marginally better until he thought about what he had to do next—tell Richard's wife her husband was dead. He'd have to get there soon, before the media got hold of this and she heard it on the television.

PICKING HERSELF UP, Lily followed Gage across the rocks and into the woods. The air wasn't really cold but her skin and shirt were wet, and when a little breeze came up, she began to shiver.

As her teeth started to chatter, Gage slung his arm around her shoulder.

"Okay?"

"Yes," she lied.

Like refugees from a shipwreck, they staggered through the woods. The fog was lifting, and she saw that this patch of ground had been left natural with thick underbrush blocking their way.

As they detoured around a tangle of brambles, thorns and twigs scratched against her skin, and she winced.

Gage pulled her closer against his side. "We need some clothes."

She nodded.

Just as they reached a dirt road hemmed in by low vegetation, a roar rose above them.

The chopper was coming back, widening its search.

Gage cursed and grabbed her hand, urging her down into a tangle of honeysuckle and blackberry bushes, the underbrush inflicting more scratches on her naked legs and thighs. Quickly, he pulled part of the vines over their heads and shoulders, trying to obscure the view from above.

Gage leaned over her, and she realized he was trying to cover her body with his.

"No," she whispered. "I've got the dark shirt. They can see your back easier than mine."

"Yeah." He shifted his position, letting her lean over him while the chopper swung back and forth in the air above them.

As she huddled under the vines, Lily couldn't help feeling as if a bull's-eye was painted on her back.

Gage pressed his cheek against her shoulder. "Relax."

"I can't. What if they land? What if they start beating the bushes for us?" she asked, hearing the quavering sound of her own voice.

He kept his own tone steady. "Where the hell would they land? On the water? If they see us, they've got to call it in."

"Or start shooting," she couldn't help adding.

"They won't," he muttered, but this time he sounded less sure.

She wanted to look up and see if the chopper was hovering directly over them. But she struggled not to move, not to give away their position.

WHEN RAND heard someone running toward him through the woods, he tensed, then saw that the paramedics had finally arrived.

He eyed the two young men with anger. "You're too late," he spat out.

"We got here as fast as we could."

"Forget it. I don't want to hear your excuses. A cop died today. A good man. One of the best." Whirling, he stalked away toward his vehicle.

Before he reached the car, one of the uniformed officers came forward. It was obvious that the man hadn't wanted to approach while Rand was with Richard.

"Sir?"

"He's dead."

"I'm sorry," the man answered perfunctorily. Well, what could he say, after all? He hadn't had the privilege of knowing Richard Francis as a friend and trusted colleague.

The officer got right back to business. "The tent's empty. But it looks like the wife was there. She left her bra on top of the sleeping bag."

Her bra? Apparently Lily Darnell wasn't here under duress this time. He'd bet that the minute she'd slipped out of her parents' house, she'd headed for her husband's camp.

Had she known all along where to find Darnell—and only been waiting for her chance to hook up? Or had she guessed where he might be and taken a chance?

Either way, they'd been cozied up here. And when she'd taken off, she hadn't bothered to get dressed. Rand pictured her running through the woods half-naked. Why?

Suddenly, the reason popped into his head.

"The river. That's where they went. Into the water."

He was thinking aloud now. "Darnell must have had an escape plan. He wouldn't try to swim across the river, would he?" With a sudden feeling of hope, he looked at the cop. "Get teams over to the estates on the left and right. We've still got a chance to nail him."

THE CHOPPER sped off, and Gage stood. He was almost naked and covered with scratches that stung his back, chest and legs. But he didn't stop to inspect the damage.

"Come on. We've got to hurry."

"Do you think they saw us?"

"It doesn't matter. They'll search for us here," he answered, then was sorry about the harsh assessment when he saw the way Lily's face contorted.

He led Lily confidently up the road as though he knew exactly where he was going, while his gaze darted around the woods, searching desperately for landmarks. He'd come here by the land route, not by the river. So he didn't even know exactly where he was.

Finally, to his vast relief, he saw a tree that had blown over in the wind but was still being held up by surrounding pines. Looking at the configuration, he breathed out a sigh.

"What?" Lily asked.

"Nothing." He left the road, forging through the underbrush, acquiring more scratches as he went, until he saw the car, partially hidden by more brambles. He picked up his pace.

That was when he heard the sound of a vehicle speeding toward them along the dirt road.

Chapter Twelve

Gage felt Lily grab his arm.

"Is that the cops?"

"It's not the welcoming committee," he snapped, then immediately apologized. "Sorry. I'm kind of tense."

"We both are."

With the new skills he'd acquired, he popped the locks on the car doors. Lily was already at the passenger door. When she heard the latch open, she slipped into the front seat while he opened the trunk and threw the bag of electronics equipment inside.

Although they were still both wet and half naked, he drove out of the hiding place, then plowed through a gap in the trees and hit another narrow road. Hidden behind a screen of leaves, they watched a police car speed by. When it had disappeared, they turned in the other direction.

"That road ends in about a mile, and they'll come back this way," Gage muttered.

"Then where are we going?" Lily asked.

"Along the river," he answered, hoping the cops hadn't had time to block all the exits to the property.

Emerging from the woods, he made a sharp left, then drove onto a manicured lawn that swooped down to the water. The wide-open space made him feel like a moving target, but he had no choice. If they didn't make it out of here in the next few minutes, the game was up.

As he drove, he thought about the gunfire they'd both heard. The cops had been shooting at somebody. Did they think it was him? Or had the cops fought it out with each other?

He hoped not, because if one of them had gotten shot, that meant all bets were off for Gage Darnell.

He made it to the other side of a sprawling white house, then found the way blocked by a couple of cars. They were either a roadblock or a row of vehicles that belonged to the property owner.

Lily gulped, as she saw the barrier.

"Duck," he ordered.

She did as he asked, and he crouched as low as he could, angling to the right. When no one popped up with guns blazing, he breathed out a sigh.

"It's not the cops," he told Lily as he squeezed through a small gap between one of the cars and a privet hedge, the mirror catching on a branch as he eased past. He kept going, hearing the branch crack as the car made it to the unobstructed part of the driveway.

Hands fused to the wheel, he headed past the house and onto a blacktop road.

It looked like they were in the clear, until a patrol car came speeding toward them with the lights flashing, obviously responding to an emergency call.

Lily gasped.

"Get down again," he shouted. "So they don't see us together."

Once more, she folded down in her seat, and he kept driving at a normal pace, figuring that the cops didn't know anybody had gotten away yet. They also didn't know what vehicle he was driving.

To his everlasting relief, the car whizzed by. He kept going down the highway, then turned off into a residential neighborhood, making several turns through the development until he came to what had been a pine forest.

A construction company had begun clearing the sandy soil, bulldozing trees and brush and leaving the mess in huge piles. But nobody was on the scene. He pulled off into one of the cleared areas, then got out to retrieve the bag of clothes he'd left in the trunk.

He gave Lily a dry T-shirt and a pair of sweat-pants. While she wiggled into them, he pulled on clothes and tennis shoes.

"Sorry, I didn't bring any shoes that will fit you," he said as they both climbed back into the car.

"You didn't know I was coming," she answered, then swung her head toward him. "Thanks for getting us out of there."

"You still have the option of turning yourself in. If you show up at the Maryland State Police barracks, you can get inside before anybody knows who you are."

"No."

Digging under the clothing still in the bag, he took out a wad of cash and shoved it into his pocket.

He was still marveling that they'd escaped from Oak Lawn. He wanted to fold his arms over the steering wheel, pillow his head against them and just rest for a few minutes. But Lily was sitting beside him, and he didn't want her to think he'd just about reached the end of his rope.

So he sat staring at the woods.

When he felt her hand on his shoulder, he turned, and she held out her arms.

He heard a strangled sound rise in his throat as he hauled her against himself and clung.

She held on just as tightly, stroking his back, then turning her face for a quick, hard kiss.

"I wouldn't have gotten out of there without you," she whispered.

"You wouldn't have been in trouble without me," he answered.

She clenched her hands on his arms. "Don't."

He swallowed and sat up straighter. "We can't stay here."

"Where are we going?"

Where, indeed? Not across the Bay Bridge. There would be cops watching the road to the mainland. But there would also be cops scouring the local area.

Still, maybe it made sense to head toward the bridge. There were a lot of shopping centers up that way where they could lose themselves in the crowd.

"With them looking for us, you need to change your appearance," he said to Lily. "Is there some kind of temporary coloring you can spray on your hair?"

"I think so."

"By now, they know we're together, so lie down in the backseat, and it'll look like I'm alone."

She climbed into the back while he drove toward Kent Narrows.

After passing several shopping centers, he stopped at one with a drugstore open early and pulled up near the entrance.

"I'd go in," he told her, "but I don't know what kind of dye to get. Or shoes."

"I'd better do it."

He handed her some of his cash. "You want to be in and out of there as fast as you can. But don't draw attention to yourself."

Her face looked pale, but her mouth was firm as she climbed quickly out of the car and hurried toward the store.

When she disappeared from sight, he turned on the radio to a music station, hoping to distract himself. To his relief, she was back in six minutes.

"Lightning speed."

She grinned. "Yeah. It's not busy at this hour of the morning."

As he drove away, she pulled out the cheap tennis shoes and socks she'd bought.

"Can you cut your hair?" he asked.

"Maybe you should do it."

He looked at the tangles she'd acquired during the swim. "I should have told you to get a hairbrush."

"I did." As they drove, she sat low behind him, smoothing the tangles out of her shoulder-length hair and staring straight ahead.

Along the highway, he parked around the back of a seafood restaurant that had gone out of business. They both climbed out.

He came around to her side, lifting a lock of her still-damp hair and running his fingers regretfully along the length. Before she could change her mind, he chopped off three inches, cringing inside as he watched her beautiful blond hair fall to the blacktop.

The first cut was the worst. He kept going, working his way from the center back to the front—when the music cut off on the radio.

"We interrupt our regular programing with a special news report."

His hand stopped in mid cut.

"They're probably announcing we're on the run," he muttered.

"Yes."

When he heard the words, "A detective with the Maryland State Police has been killed in a shootout with dangerous fugitives Gage and Lily Darnell," he went rigid.

Lily whirled toward the radio, her eyes wide. "What?"

He waved her to silence. "Quiet."

Fighting a feeling of déjà vu, he reached inside the car and turned up the volume.

"Darnell and his wife should be considered

armed and dangerous. Darnell is six feet, one eighty pounds, dark hair and dark eyes. His wife is five feet five, blond, blue eyes. At the time of the shooting, Darnell was on the run from a previous murder charge. Do not approach the couple."

The report went on. "The police will release the name of the slain detective after his family has been notified."

When the regular programing resumed, Gage slammed his fists against the side of the car, pain radiating from his knuckles.

"Two detectives came to our house—Rand McClellan and Richard Francis," Lily murmured. "And they showed up again at the Wilson estate."

"It's probably one of them."

She nodded. "Yes."

"When I heard the shots back at Oak Lawn, I didn't know what to think. Now one of the detectives is dead and somebody's trying to pin it on me."

Lily looked around as though she expected a police car to pull up next to them in the parking lot, and cops jumping out with guns blazing. "We have to get out of town," she breathed. "Before they box us in."

He gave her a fierce look. "I'm not leaving."

"Every cop on the Eastern Shore will be looking for us."

"Uh-huh."

"Then…"

"You can clear out. I have to find out what happened when they stormed the campsite. I'm not going to let them make me a scapegoat again. Lily, I've got *two* murder charges hanging over me."

She took her lower lip between her teeth.

He felt a stab of pain as a new possibility struck him. "What? You think I killed that detective while you were hightailing it for the river?"

"Of course not!"

"But you're thinking that there's not much chance of ever clearing myself."

"I didn't say that." She looked down at her hands.

"You'd better leave. I won't drag you down with me."

She raised her gaze to his. "I'm not going to leave you." Brushing her fingers across the side of her hair that he'd chopped off, she added, "Besides, you need to finish the cutting job or I'm going to look like I ran into a crazed beautician."

It was a poor attempt at a joke, but he managed a small grin. Their gazes locked for several heartbeats, then she turned away and he began to cut her hair again, silently struggling to hold his hand steady.

Grimly, he worked the scissors, trying to keep

from making a mess of her hair. He felt like that cartoon character with the dark cloud hanging over his head. Only Lily was standing out in the storm with him—and he couldn't even insist that she go back home. He was sure they already knew that he hadn't kidnapped his wife this time. Or if he had, she'd changed sides pretty quickly.

"Sorry," he muttered.

"Maybe I'm the one who led them to you," she said in a barely audible voice.

He wanted to issue a denial, but that could be true. Instead he kept working, feeling the tension between them was thick enough to cut with the scissors.

"How is it?" she said when he stepped back.

"Fine," he answered automatically.

She picked up the can of spray dye she'd bought and bent over so she could look in the side mirror. She gave her hair a tentative spritz of brown spray and used the brush to work it in.

Glancing up, she asked, "How do I look?"

"I hear blondes have more fun."

LILY WORKED more brown into her hair, stopping to inspect the results in the car's side mirror.

Not very professional, but it was the best she could do out here in the parking lot.

After the radio announcement, she was feeling numb, and she needed to sit down. But when she saw that Gage was cleaning up the blacktop, she turned to help him. Getting down on her knees, she swept up clumps of blond hair with her hands.

"We've got most of it. At least I don't think a casual passerby will notice anything," Gage muttered.

"I'll bet the birds will take the rest of it away for nests," she answered.

"Right. Our good deed for the day."

She could see he was struggling for calm, so she took the hair to a wooded area and scattered it around. When she came back, he cleared his throat. "If I could get you out of danger, I would. As things stand now, if the cops catch us, you could get hurt."

Hurt. Or killed. He hadn't said it, but she read it between the lines.

She folded her arms across her chest, feeling the chilled skin.

"We need to get off the streets, and the cops will be checking the motels," Gage said. "I had been trying to avoid breaking the law too much, but now…" He sighed. "The beach is the perfect place for breaking and entering, with renters moving in and out. Plus, this is after the end of the season, so there should be vacant properties. We can look for isolated beach houses that are empty."

"Okay," she agreed.

He looked surprised that she hadn't given him an argument, but she was still trying to think through what had happened.

"You know more about this than I do. I'll try not to get in the way," she said in a low voice.

She'd wanted him to say she wasn't in the way. But he only nodded and went back to the trunk. When he reappeared, he was wearing a backward baseball cap. It didn't hide his face, but the salt-and-pepper wig sticking out below the cap made him look like an entirely different guy. The sunglasses he donned added to the easy transformation.

She felt her jaw drop as she stared at him. "I wouldn't know you. Were did you get the wig?"

"One of those dollar stores they have all over the place around here."

They drove away from the restaurant and into an area where the lots were fairly large.

"Look for closed blinds, no cars." Gage advised. "If possible, we'd like an area where the neighbors aren't home, either."

After a half hour, they found a house he thought was suitable.

"Wait here," Gage said after driving around the back.

He watched Lily lean back against the seat and close her eyes. She looked whipped.

But why not? The last two hours had been pretty traumatic. He was wrung out, too, but he knew he couldn't rest yet.

Glancing back, he saw her pale face. He wished she'd protest about breaking into another house. Really, he wished she'd tell him she was going back to Baltimore where her parents would hide her. But she only sat there, feigning sleep.

Was she upset enough that he could persuade her to get on a plane out of the country? But she'd need a passport for that. He could probably get her one under a false name, but that would take up valuable time.

He sighed. He'd wanted her with him, now he'd gotten his wish, and it wasn't working out the way he'd thought.

Trying not to clench his jaw, he walked to the back door and put his hand on the knob, sending his mind into the lock. Now that he had some experience manipulating the physical world, the sensation was becoming familiar.

He stopped just inside the front door, listening. Then he walked rapidly around the house, making sure that every room was empty. The place was a typical upscale furnished beach house with most of the living area on the second floor. There were five bedrooms, a great room next to an open kitchen, a partial view of the river and a hot tub on the deck.

He felt a spurt of elation when he saw the bright yellow card by the phone. Someone had left a welcome note for the next rental occupants—for three weeks from the present date.

Elation was followed by guilt as he thought about how quickly his values had changed. He was the owner of a security company, for Lord's sake. Now breaking into other people's property was as routine as installing alarm systems.

LILY KEPT her head turned toward the door, waiting for Gage to reappear and praying that he hadn't run into any trouble.

She told herself that he was just being thorough. But she couldn't relax until she saw him open the door and amble back to the car as though he had nothing better to do than enjoy a vacation on the Eastern Shore.

"Nobody's going to be here for the next three weeks," he informed her.

"Good," she answered, praying they wouldn't

be there for anywhere near that long. On the other hand, what was the alternative?

Did she really think that Gage could clear his name in the next few weeks? Every time he made a move, the situation went farther downhill. And she'd only made things worse by showing up.

When she saw he was watching her, she climbed out of the car and picked up the duffel bag, then headed for the house while Gage brought in his equipment. In the main bathroom, she used the facilities. Then, because she wanted to be alone for a while, she evened up the ends of her hair and worked in some more brown dye.

As she fussed with her hair, she tried to figure out what to do. Was it better to stay with him, or would he have a better chance on his own?

Slowly she walked back to the great room. It was dark and silent, and she felt a stab of panic.

Had he led her, then cut and run—

For her own good?

When she heard the door open and close on the entry level, she felt a surge of relief. Hurrying to the railing, she saw Gage standing in the lower hall, his shoulders slumped.

In that moment, he didn't look like the Gage

Darnell she'd always known. He'd always been upbeat. Sure of himself and sure of his goals. Not now.

As if he sensed she was watching, he looked up and saw her, then straightened. Briskly he walked up the stairs.

"How do you like the kitchen?" he asked.

"It's fine," she said, even though she'd hardly given it a glance.

"I know a good kitchen is important to you."

"Something else is on your mind," she said quietly.

She watched him shift his weight from one foot to the other.

"Nothing. I mean…well, I checked the house. There's no computer. And I need one to hack into the Cranesbrook system." He scuffed his foot against the tile floor. "I could buy one, but it's safer for you to go out. Are you willing to do it?"

Instead of giving him a direct answer, she said, "Computers aren't exactly my strong suit. What am I supposed to buy, and where do I get it?"

"Your best bet is probably a big-box office-supply store. We passed a couple between here and the drugstore. Just get whatever they've got on sale."

When he started ticking off the specifications, she stopped him. "Write it down."

He picked up the pad beside the phone and began making a list.

She watched him for a minute, then restlessly started opening kitchen cabinets. There were enough pots and pans and utensils to put together a decent meal. And the previous renters had left some basic supplies.

"Here," he said, holding out the pad.

"Do we have enough cash to pay for a computer?" she asked.

"These days you can get all that for under a thousand dollars," he said, giving her another wad of cash. "And if you can find a deal that includes a black-and-white printer, get it. I don't care about durability. We're not going to need it for long."

She turned toward the door, then stopped as she realized she might not be going anywhere. "I can't start the car with my mind. Do you happen to have a key?"

"Yeah. There was one in a magnetic box under the right front fender. It's in the glove compartment now." He gave her a key to the house, which was in the drawer under the phone, then walked outside with her.

Before she climbed into the car, he put his hand on her shoulder. "Maybe it's not such a good idea for you to go out," he muttered.

"I'm fine," she lied, then reached for him.

He gave her a hard kiss, and she clung to him for heartbeats before easing away and inserting the key in the ignition.

As she pulled away, she knew the time had come to make a major decision. Return to this house and Gage—or drive away and not come back.

Chapter Thirteen

Lily headed toward the Bay Bridge, wondering if she should keep going and take her chances back in Baltimore. Assuming they didn't have a roadblock there by now.

She'd thought she was so clever switching places with Pam so she could go look for Gage. Then she'd found him—and led the police right to his hiding place.

Was she going to keep making things worse by sticking around? If so, she should clear out.

If she stayed, she wanted to help Gage—not get him arrested.

Well, he'd given her a job to do. He needed the computer, and she was going to buy it for him—without getting into trouble.

After pulling into the parking lot of the office-supply store, she took several deep breaths, then climbed out of the car. Inside, she played the part of a ditz-brained housewife who had saved up to buy the family their first computer.

The young sales clerk was glad to steer her through the purchasing process, unaware he was dealing with a woman wanted for the murder of a police detective.

By the time she'd paid for the machine and gotten a staffer to load it in the car, she was feeling a few degrees more confident, so she made a quick stop at a discount department store and bought some clothing. After changing in a dressing room, she made one more stop—at a grocery store, where she bought breakfast food and the ingredients of a simple meal she knew Gage loved—steak, baked potatoes and salad.

She was hurrying to the express checkout line, when she realized she'd pushed her luck one beat too far.

A uniformed police officer was standing at the front of the store, scanning the crowd. And she knew that he wasn't there by accident. He was looking for the fugitives.

The cop's gaze swung toward her, and she forgot to breathe normally as he gave her a once-over, then scanned the other shoppers. Well, here was where she found out if her new haircut and dye job passed inspection.

Hoping she didn't look as though her heart was pounding inside her chest, she stepped into the shortest line and waited until she reached the checker.

Once she'd paid for her purchases, she walked smartly to the exit, put her groceries in the backseat of her stolen car and drove straight to the beach house, with a better appreciation of what Gage's life had been like for the past two weeks.

Because the computer was heavy, she left it in the car and carried her other purchases inside.

When she came up the stairs to the great room, Gage was sitting on the sofa staring at the television. He was watching CNN, and she went rigid when she saw that the Eastern Shore murder had made the national news.

Apparently he wasn't aware that she'd entered the room, because he didn't turn. He was staring at his photograph on the screen.

She set down her bags at the top of the steps. She might have gone right to Gage, but she was stopped in her tracks as she saw her own face flash on the screen.

The next picture was of a man in a business suit. Richard Francis. The announcer said he had been shot and killed while trying to apprehend the dangerous Darnell couple. Nobody at the site had actually seen Darnell and his wife, but evidence inside the tent suggested that they'd been camping there.

When she heard that bit of news, Lily winced, and Gage whirled around, the Sig in his hand.

She went stock-still when she saw the weapon pointed at her.

Cursing, he set the gun on the coffee table. "Sorry, I'm a little jumpy."

She gave a small nod, then gestured toward the TV. "I guess it wouldn't have done much good to clear out of the area."

"This is the modern era with the twenty-minute news cycle where a juicy local story leaps into the national spotlight. Like that woman who rescued her husband when he was being transported from court to jail and they killed a cop in the process."

"We didn't kill anyone."

"Let's hope we can prove it," he said, his voice grim.

She walked past him and picked up the remote control from the coffee table.

"I think we've had enough television," she murmured. After shutting off the set, she turned back to Gage and took in the bleak look on his face.

"What's wrong? Did something else happen?"

He looked down at his hands, then back at her.

"You were gone a long time. I thought maybe you weren't coming back," he said, his voice gritty.

"I thought about leaving," she whispered.

"I understand why you wouldn't want to stick with a murder suspect."

"Lord, Gage, that's not it at all."

"Then what?"

"I was feeling like I screwed things up for you. I was thinking that if I'd never come looking for you, you'd be a lot better off now."

"No!" She saw him swallow hard. "It means a lot to me that you wanted to be with me. A hell of a lot," he said, his voice full of emotion. "It wasn't your fault how it turned out."

She could have debated the point, but he didn't let her. He was seven feet away from her, and he didn't get up from the couch, but she felt something like the touch of his fingertips against her hair, sweeping loose strands gently back from her face.

Her eyes widened. "Gage?"

He shifted on the couch, pressing his palms against the cushions, but he continued to stare intently at her. Then she sensed unseen fingers moving from her hair to her cheek.

In response, she leaned her head to the side, returning the pressure, her gaze never leaving Gage's face.

The tactile communication was very strange and very unique, yet at this moment it felt so right. She'd felt a strain between them since they'd left the campground. Now her husband was reaching out to her in a way that nobody had ever experienced before.

She opened her mouth to puff out a breath, and the touch shifted to her lips, tracing their shape, then lining the inner edge.

"How are you doing that?" she whispered, even when she really knew the answer.

"With my mind. I've been practicing to see what kinds of things I can do and feel. I'm getting more control over my power."

"Oh."

She saw a wicked look cross his features just before he shifted the focus of his attention and the way he was touching her. He'd been using unseen fingers to caress her. Suddenly she felt the stroke of his tongue against hers. In response, a thrill of sexual arousal shivered through her. Swaying on her feet, she reached back and steadied herself against the back of the recliner that was angled toward the television.

The intensity of Gage's gaze stunned her. "What does it feel like to you?" she managed to ask.

He gave her a look that melted her bones. "Like

I'm kissing you. Deeply, hotly," he answered, his voice thick.

She tried to take that in, then abandoned the intellectual exercise when the front of her shirt stirred. Her gaze shot to him, and she saw that his face had taken on a look of concentration. When she glanced down, she saw the top button of her shirt slide slowly open.

The next button followed and the next, until the shirt was completely undone. Then, as though he were standing right in front of her, he brushed the sides of the shirt slowly back, dragging the fabric against her skin as they moved.

She hadn't bothered to put on a bra, so the action bared her breasts to Gage's view.

She saw him swallow hard, saw his hands press more tightly against the sofa cushions as he stared at her.

"Beautiful," he murmured. "And so soft, so sexy."

She felt unseen hands cup her breasts, lifting and cradling them as though he held them in his palms.

The breath rushed out of her lungs. Then she felt that his thumbs were making a circuit around each of her nipples, drawing that contracted smaller and smaller circles until they stroked against the sides of the raised centers.

Gage gained confidence in this new seduction

method every moment he continued. Skillfully, he plucked at the distended tips, and she couldn't hold back a moan as unbearable arousal fired her blood.

He was still across the room, and he was making her so hot that she could barely breathe.

Her gaze locked with Gage's as the shirt slicked back off her shoulders, holding her arms captive.

The arousal on his face took her breath away. He looked as though he wanted to eat her alive.

As she stood there with the top of her body exposed to his view, the zipper at the front of her shorts lowered, and the shorts pushed down her legs, along with the panties she'd purchased at the department store.

All her hidden, feminine places were totally exposed now. Her shorts trapped her feet and her shirt bound her arms. Gage held her captive as effectively as if he'd lassoed her arms and feet. Only he hadn't used a rope. He'd done it totally with his mind.

"I think you have me at an unfair advantage," she managed.

"Yeah."

When he stood up, she felt a surge of heat as she saw the erection straining at the front of his jeans.

When she swayed on her feet, he quickly rounded the coffee table and gathered her into his arms.

He had turned her on almost beyond endurance without any real physical contact. Now he lowered his head to hers, devouring her mouth in a hot, urgent kiss, the hair of his new beard scraping her face. As he pulled her into his arms, she felt his erection wedged between them.

When the kiss broke, they were both gasping for air. She struggled to speak. "My arms. Get the sleeves off my arms."

His hands and perhaps his mind, too, tore at the sleeves, and when he freed her, she immediately reached for the snap at the front of his jeans.

He had undressed her from afar, but she had no such talents.

Still it took only seconds to lower his zipper and free him from his jeans. They both made a sound of satisfaction as she took him in her hand.

When she had kicked away her shorts, he rid himself of his remaining clothing, and they fell together to the rug. He gathered her to him, rocking with her in a fury of need. He ended up on top of her, and she opened her legs, reaching to guide him inside her.

He plunged home, wringing a glad cry from her. And they both began to move, urgency driving them.

The intensity was too great to last. She

climaxed in a roiling explosion of ecstasy, then felt him follow her over the edge.

They ended in a sweaty tangle on the rug, both breathing hard.

"Don't leave me again," she gasped.

He raised his head and looked down at her. "I thought *you* had left *me*."

"I'm here. I'll always be here."

She reached for him again, her arms locking around his back. She'd told herself she had to be strong, but suddenly it was impossible to hold herself together. When she started to cry, he stroked her hair the way he'd done from across the room.

She struggled to get control of herself, because they were in too much danger for her to fall to pieces.

"I'm okay," she managed.

"This is more than anyone should have to endure."

"We can do it. Together."

"I hope so."

She allowed herself a few more moments in his arms, then raised her head. "I got the computer," she said, because she felt that they needed to start doing something positive to prove they were innocent.

"Good."

"You want me to fix breakfast or lunch?" she asked.

"Lunch."

He eased away from her, and she watched him collect his clothing before exiting the house.

RAND MCCLELLAN looked up as one of the task-force men stepped into the squad room.

"I suppose you don't have any word on Darnell?" he asked.

The man shook his head. "Sorry. I know you're anxious to find him. But I think he's long gone from the area. I would be, if I were wanted for two murders. We've got the highway patrol and the local cops looking for him in all nearby states. And we've got men at BWI and Reagan National."

Rand sighed. Somehow he didn't think that was going to be enough. Darnell was a tricky bastard to have eluded capture this long. It made sense for him to have long since cleared out of the area. But what if he was sticking around because that was exactly what he *wouldn't* be expected to do?"

"Just in case, we're checking local motels," the officer said.

Rand nodded while he pondered Gage Darnell's options, trying to duplicate the man's thinking. Motels were too obvious for a guy who had been camping out with a fair amount of expensive equipment. Where had he gotten the money for that? And what was he going to try next?

An idea struck Rand, and for the first time since Richard's death, he felt a surge of optimism.

"I'd like a list of rental properties available in the area."

WHILE GAGE started setting up the computer in one of the spare bedrooms, Lily put the potatoes into the oven. When they were almost done, she started the steaks.

Gage came into the kitchen when they had been broiling for several minutes.

"That smells wonderful. I'm starved." He gave her a wicked look. "Nothing like hot sex to spur the appetite."

She grinned at him, as if they were here on vacation with nothing better to do than enjoy some quality time together.

"I'll set the table." He opened drawers, finding cutlery, and she watched him, thinking how wonderful this simple afternoon was. They'd been apart for months, and now they were living like man and wife again. It felt very real—and very precious because she knew that it could all be snatched away from them so easily.

Turning quickly, she clamped her teeth

together, ordering herself not to start crying again. By the time the steak was finished broiling, she had herself under control.

Normal. Act normal.

"So what does that look on your face mean?" he asked as they sat across from each other.

"I was thinking how strange this situation is. We're sitting down to lunch like a regular couple on a Saturday afternoon. But you have a beard and need a haircut. I've got a haircut and a dye job," she said, trying to keep it light.

"And the police could come busting through the door," he added.

"Let's not spoil the mood."

"Yeah. Sorry."

He cut a piece of steak. She did too, chewing and swallowing before asking, "So what are you planning to do with the computer?"

"Well, I tried to break into Cranesbrook in person," he answered in a conversational tone. "And it didn't work."

She almost choked on the piece of meat she was eating. "What happened?"

"I couldn't get in. They'd increased the security. They've got something to hide, and I want to find out what it is."

She wondered if it had been as cut and dried as

that, or if he'd had another harrowing escape. Probably to keep her from asking for details, he started speaking again.

"So I'm going to try and hack into their system."

"Have you had any experience with that?"

He looked slightly embarrassed. "As a teenager, I got into trouble for hacking into the school computer."

"Oh, yeah?"

"I altered my grade in a computer class. The teacher gave me a B and I wanted to prove that I should have gotten an A."

"Did it work?"

"Mr. Westhaver was mad as hell. So I guess not."

"Did you do other hacking?"

"It's better if you don't know."

She struggled to repress the grin playing around her lips. "Well, it sounds like you have the skills to tackle Cranesbrook. What are you looking for exactly?"

He made an exasperated sound. "I wish I knew. I was working at the damn place for months, and I didn't know anything strange was going on in the lab. For starters, I'd like to know about the chemical I was exposed to. Was it an official project or something a scientist was cooking up on his own?"

While she had him talking, she figured she didn't have anything to lose by asking some more questions.

"When we left the campground, you had a bunch of equipment with you."

"Yeah."

"What is all that?"

"I've been designing some specialized security devices. Stuff that works without hard wires, like a wireless computer network. That's how I knew when you showed up and where you were. The same with the police. The whole system is tied into a portable GPS device."

"And that got ruined in the water?"

"Yeah, but I had another one in the case with my equipment."

She'd gotten him distracted from their primary problem, and she was glad to see the old Gage enthusiastically telling her about the inventions that he was perfecting. Not just an alarm system, but miniaturized transmission equipment.

She didn't understand the technical details, but she loved watching his face as he talked about his work. For months he'd been keeping his intellectual life to himself. Now she was feeling more like his marriage partner again.

After lunch, Gage started to help her clean up

the kitchen, but she knew he was anxious to get back to the computer.

"You go back to work," she told him. "The sooner you get into the Cranesbrook computers, the better."

He disappeared into the bedroom again.

At first, she heard curses drifting down the hall, and she figured it was better to give him some space.

When she didn't hear anything from Gage for over an hour, she finally popped her head in the door.

He was leaning intently toward the computer screen, reading a spreadsheet.

"You found something?" she asked.

He looked disgusted. "Not much. But I do know the work in Lab 7 is something called Project Cypress."

"What is it?"

"I'm not sure. Maybe someone wasn't using correct safety procedures and a dangerous chemical was released in the explosion. And now that someone is trying to cover it up by making sure I can't talk about what happened."

"Or maybe the program is screwed up, and they're looking for a way to explain why it got off track. An explosion in the lab would do the trick. You just rushed in at the wrong time."

"Unfortunately, those theories still leave a lot of loose ends. Like, for example, the explosion came from the closet. Which makes it sound like someone was storing dangerous chemicals improperly."

"Unless the accident was deliberate."

He grimaced. "Yeah."

She sat down in the chair in the corner, watching him work. An hour later, he sighed. "It looks like they just didn't leave a paper trail."

"But you were a witness. Which makes you a big problem to them. If you're on the loose, you can testify about what happened."

When Gage bent to the computer again, she leaned back in the chair and closed her eyes. Gage had uncovered some interesting information, but it wasn't going to prove he hadn't murdered anyone.

That was going to take getting back into Cranesbrook, and she began working out a plan for how they were going to do it, although she was pretty sure Gage wasn't going to fall in line with her ideas.

"We have to figure out the most likely person to have ordered you confined to that mental hospital where you couldn't talk to anyone," she said.

"It could be Nelson Ulrich, but I'm putting my money on Sid Edmonston."

"Why?"

"He came down here from their facility in New

Jersey just before the lab accident, and he's stayed down here—to keep tabs on the manhunt, among other things. When I run into barriers in the computer files, they seem to be coming from his office. Also, he's got the money to hire Dr. Morton to keep me and Vanderhoven under wraps." Gage waved his arm in exasperation. "But he could be working with Bray for all I know!"

She took her lower lip between her teeth. Bray and Gage had been more than partners. In the Special Forces, they had put their lives in each other's hands. "Is that what you really think?" she asked in a barely audible voice.

He pressed his lips together, then answered. "I don't know. If Bray isn't in on this, why is he missing?"

"We have to get Edmonston to talk."

"Oh, sure."

"I have an idea."

He gave her a long look. "I don't like the sound of that. You're thinking about something dangerous."

"Tell me about your covert transmission equipment."

He shifted in his seat. "Tell me what you have in mind."

"You first," she insisted. "Is it operational?"

She could see him making mental evaluations. "Almost. Why do you want to know?"

"Maybe we'd better start conducting some tests to see."

He tipped his head to one side, looking at her. "I sense a bout of the famous Lily Darnell creativity coming on."

Despite the circumstances, she grinned. "Yeah, you do."

Chapter Fourteen

Tossing and turning in his bed, Rand McClellan tried to escape the dream. But he couldn't get away.

Sweat broke out on his brow. He and Richard had thought they were so clever. They'd tracked Gage Darnell to a beach house and taken up positions near the front and back doors. Then everything went wrong. When they called out to Darnell that he was surrounded, he came out shooting, an automatic weapon in each hand.

Then the scene switched and they were in the woods, back at the campground, and Gage Darnell was chasing them. Now, somehow, he had *two* guns in each hand, and he kept firing like the mechanical monster from *The Terminator.*

Rand knew in his gut that everything was going wrong. He and Richard had somehow lost their weapons. They couldn't return fire. All they could do was run for their lives with the monster pounding behind them, getting closer and closer.

He knew what was going to happen. Richard was going to die. And there wasn't a damn thing he could do about it. Then he'd be next.

The son of a bitch would get him, too.

He moaned, trying to make it come out differently.

"Wake up. You're having a bad dream."

The voice shocked him out of slumber. But not out of the nightmare.

Someone was in the bedroom. And the voice grated along his nerve endings.

For a moment longer, he feigned sleep, then opened his eyes and whipped toward the drawer of the bedside table.

The voice that had awakened him stopped him in mid reach. "Don't do anything stupid like pulling out that gun. You don't want to end up dead. If I kill you, I'll never get a chance to prove my innocence."

Rand flopped back against the wrinkled pillows and stared up at the figure looming over his bed. It was Gage Darnell.

He'd considered the possibility that Darnell would come after him, and he'd made sure the doors and windows were securely locked and the alarm had been set.

"How did you get in here?"

Darnell stood very still in a shaft of light coming from the hallway, making it impossible to see his face. "I'm a hardened criminal. I have my ways."

"Right. A hardened criminal. You killed Richard. Now you've come to kill me."

"Wrong. I've come to convince you I didn't have anything to do with your partner's death."

Rand gave a harsh laugh. "Innocent. That's what they all say."

"I know. But in this case, it's true."

"If you want to prove you're innocent, turn yourself in."

Darnell made a derisive sound. "Oh, sure. I can really be effective sitting in a cell."

"That's better then getting killed in a shootout. They haven't executed a murderer in Maryland in years."

"Thanks. But I don't plan for it to end that way. Turn on the bedside light so we can see each other better."

Rand was scrambling for a way to take the bastard. Meanwhile, he complied, then watched as Darnell sat down in the easy chair in the corner.

He looked relaxed, but the gun pointed at Rand's chest said otherwise. "I assume you have a make on the bullet that killed your partner," he said.

"Yeah."

"What gun did it come from?"

"Why should I tell you?"

"What do you have to lose?" Darnell asked, his voice very calm.

Rand's lips hardened. "A Sig P220 Sport."

"That's interesting. You think I'd choose a sports pistol or one that's easy on the kickback? You think I'm not strong enough or experienced enough for the standard model?"

"Maybe your wife did it."

"You sick bastard." Darnell started to stand, and Rand felt a jolt of fear. He'd been angry enough to say the wrong thing. Darnell might be a killer, but he cared about his wife.

The intruder looked like he was struggling for control. Very deliberately he sat down again. "Lily wouldn't shoot anyone," he said, his voice hard.

Rand knew he should keep his mouth shut, but he heard himself say, "Stress makes people do things they wouldn't ordinarily consider. Like giving her tail the slip at her parents' house."

"She's not a killer."

"Either you did it or she did."

"Not true. Somebody else was at the campground. They set me up."

Rand couldn't keep the sarcasm out of his voice. "You were set up twice? How unfortunate for you."

"Let's assume it was the same person both times. Maybe we can prove it tonight."

Rand laughed. "It'll be a cold day in hell before you can do that."

"Keep an open mind. Somebody else pulled the trigger. We just have to find out who it was. How many men did you have closing in on me at the campsite, including you and your partner."

Rand hesitated, then said, "Five."

"My GPS screen showed six. There was another guy at the campsite. The shooter."

Rand didn't bother to think of a comeback. He was busy assessing his chances of getting out of this alive. He decided that for the moment, his best option was to go along with this madman who'd had the guts to break into the house of the detective who wanted to bring him down for killing his partner.

But was there any possibility of help? Rand had arranged to have a patrol car drive by his house periodically in case Darnell was stalking him.

If he stalled, would the patrol show up?

"Where have you been hiding out?" he asked in a conversational voice.

"In a beach house."

"I've been checking them. But we don't have

enough manpower to get to them all in a short amount of time."

"Lucky for me. But let's stop wasting time. Get dressed," Darnell said.

"Where are we going?"

"You'll find out pretty soon."

Rand complied. As he bent down to slip on his shoe, he spotted the book on new crime-scene techniques he'd been reading. It was lying half under the bed. He could hurl it at Darnell and hope his shot went wild.

His muscles were tensing when a sudden sound made him stop in mid reach.

"What's that?"

The sound crackled again, and Rand blinked as he heard Lily Darnell's voice.

"Are we ready?"

"Yes," Darnell answered.

Lily's voice had come from a speaker clipped to her husband's waist. Rand didn't know what he was using to speak to her because he had no obvious sending equipment.

"Have I managed to capture your interest?" he asked, speaking to Rand again.

"Yes," Rand admitted.

"Let's go, then. Because we don't want to be late for the party."

IN THE DARKNESS of the car, Lily checked the lighted dial of her watch. It was time for her performance to begin. She dialed a private number, then fought to keep her voice from quavering as she waited for the phone to ring.

When a man picked up, she said, "Is this Sidney Edmonston?"

"Who is this?" Edmonston asked, his voice thick with sleep.

"Lily Darnell."

He woke up quickly. "How did you get my private number?"

"I had to do some digging," she answered. "I want to talk to you."

"About what?"

"I'd rather not say over the phone."

He made a snorting sound. "The phone company has a record of calls."

"Yes. But I'm using a prepaid cell that only makes outgoing calls. I paid cash for it, so they can't trace it back to me."

"Very thorough."

"Can we meet at your office?" she asked, hoping the suggestion would help put him at ease.

"When?"

"What about now?"

"It's the middle of the night."

"Then we won't be disturbed. Tell the guard to let me in the front gate."

He hesitated, and she clenched her hand around the instrument, wondering if this whole plan was going up in smoke right now.

When he said, "Okay," she let the breath she'd been holding ease out of her chest.

"Give me half an hour," he added.

She looked at her watch. "I'll be at the gate at 3:30."

She was sitting in another stolen car, already within sight of the Cranesbrook gate, so she'd know if Edmonston came in alone. She should relax. She had nothing to do for half an hour. But tension crackled along her nerve endings as she waited for the president of the company to appear.

He was a few minutes early, which was a relief. Or maybe he was making sure he could set things up the way he wanted them.

He stopped at the gate and had a short conversation with the guard. Then he drove on through. She gave him six minutes to get to his office, then couldn't make herself sit there any longer.

When she pulled up to the gatehouse, her heart was thumping.

As a uniformed guard stepped out, she rolled

down her window. "Lily Darnell to see Mr. Edmonston."

"I'll have to look inside your car and in the trunk."

"Of course." She'd been expecting that. Still, her footing wasn't quite steady as she stepped out of the car. Trying to look like she had nothing to hide, she stood aside while he looked inside the car and inside the trunk, then used a flashlight and a mirror on a long pole to inspect the underside of the chassis.

Next he looked through the briefcase she'd brought along. It contained only papers and a CD.

When he found nothing incriminating, he turned to her. This was the most dangerous part of the inspection, and she fought to keep her face impassive as he patted her down for weapons.

Again, he seemed satisfied.

"The front office is in the third building on the right," the guard said. "Mr. Edmonston is waiting for you on the second floor. Turn to the right when you get off the elevator."

"Thank you," she said politely.

She climbed back into the car and when the gate opened, she drove through as if she had every right to be there.

At this hour of the morning, the Cranesbrook campus was deserted, and there were no streetlights, making the empty streets look spooky.

Lily knew where to find the administration building. She'd been there after Gage ended up in the hospital. And she had also been in Edmonston's office.

There was only one other car in the executive parking lot when she pulled up in front of the two-story brick building. It must be Edmonston's.

She hoped he was alone. But she had no control over what he chose to do now. She could only cross her fingers that her plan was going to work. It had sounded so clever when she'd explained it to Gage. Now that she was here, though, her mouth was so dry she wondered if she'd be able to speak.

Still, she climbed smartly out of the car and took a deep breath of the crisp night air. A few fall leaves had drifted onto the sidewalk, and they crunched under her feet as she marched toward the building. The front door was unlocked.

Bypassing the elevator, she walked to the stairs, then up to the second floor, hearing her footsteps echo on the concrete. The metal exit door put her in the hallway right outside Edmonston's office.

She stepped through a glass door into the reception area and saw through to his private domain, where he was sitting behind his desk, his bald head gleaming in the lamplight. His expression was quizzical as she walked through the door.

"Mrs. Darnell. I didn't expect to see you again."

She couldn't stop herself from retorting, "I'll bet."

Edmonston kept his gaze steady. "So what are you doing here?" he asked. "Did your husband send you?"

"No."

"You've been hiding out with him, haven't you?"

"Yes. But I don't want to stay with him. He's dangerous. Unstable." She gave him a look dripping with sincerity. "I don't know from one minute to the next whether he's going to kiss me or threaten to kill me."

Edmonston leaned forward. "That's interesting."

Wondering what he would say, she tried a direct question. "He got doused with a dangerous chemical in that explosion, didn't he?"

"You said you wanted to talk to me. Did you come to pump me for information?"

"No." She swallowed. "I want money."

He tipped his head to one side, studying her as though she were a lab animal in a cage. "For what?"

She held up the briefcase she'd brought. "Gage hacked into your computer system. He downloaded some information that you'd rather not have circulated. About your business."

Edmonston looked mildly interested. "Like what?"

"He found out that this part of the company is in financial trouble and that some of the men in the labs have been keeping double records."

"What men?"

"You'll have to pay me for that information."

"You might have some papers with data but Darnell made it up. Our systems are secure. Do you expect me to believe he got through our firewall?"

"He's an expert hacker."

"Thanks for telling me." Edmonston's hands had been out of sight below the level of the desk.

Suddenly he stood up, and she saw that he was holding a gun.

She gasped and took a step back.

"Stay right where you are."

Stiffening her legs to keep from falling, she waited with her breath shallow. Before she could take another step, he rounded the desk.

"You think I'd fall for your ploy? I'm not that stupid. I know he sent you. And I know you've got to be wearing a wire."

Before she could protest, he reached out with his free hand and ripped open the front of her blouse so that it hung loose over the vest she'd donned. It was made of a special padded material that was designed to hide the transmitter she was wearing.

Edmonston tore the vest away, then closed his hand around the flat plastic box beneath it.

"You think you can fool me with a trick like that?" he snarled. "Did you think you could convince me that you weren't working with Darnell?"

Dropping the device to the desk, he slammed a glass paperweight down on the plastic.

She heard the cover and the electronics within shatter. Then he pulled the wires out and tore them apart.

Lily stared in horror at the ruined transmitter that Gage had so carefully wired to her. "He said it would work," she said in a thin voice. She didn't have to fake terror. In the next few minutes, this man could kill her, and there was nothing she could do about it—except play for time.

"Too bad he underestimated me."

"Please, don't hurt me," she whimpered. "I had to do what he said. I wasn't lying about his being unstable. I'm afraid of him. Can you help me?"

"You're on your own now. He's not going to rescue you. He can't get into the compound. You're stuck," he added with a look of satisfaction. "If your husband has been poking into my business, this CD and papers aren't the only evidence. Where is the computer that he was using?"

She opened her mouth and closed it again.

"What—you think you can bargain with me?"

"Yes."

"I don't think so." When he slapped her across the face, she gasped, then fought to keep tears from blurring her vision.

Roughly, he pushed her into one of the sturdy guest chairs opposite the desk. With the gun still on her, he moved to the closet and opened a box. Inside was various equipment, including a length of rope. Not the standard issue for a corporate executive.

He wound the rope around her body and the back of the chair, holding her arms at her sides and her body in place. After her torso was secured, he tied her ankles to the chair legs. When he was finished, he stepped back and inspected his handiwork.

Satisfied that she couldn't get away, he put the gun down on the desk.

"What are you going to do?" she quavered.

"Now that I know we're not being recorded, I can be a little more candid. I'm going to kill you," he murmured. "The question is—how painful will it be?"

She lifted her chin, pretending a show of confidence she didn't feel. "You can't get away with it."

A sneer flickered on his lips. "You don't think so? I've already gotten away with it. I killed that janitor at the hospital. And I killed that cop at the campground. And—" He stopped short.

"What?"

Ignoring the question, he said, "Why do you think I can't keep up my winning streak?"

She stared at him in frozen horror. "You were at the campground?"

"Yeah. I was pretty sure Gage would be camping out, given his macho constitution. So I asked around and found out where he liked to go, then gave the cops some hints about where to find him. I followed them in the back way and shot one of the detectives. Richard Francis, to be exact."

Even as Edmonston's bragging made nausea rise in her throat, she felt a flash of relief. She'd been sick with worry that she'd drawn the cops to the campground. Edmonston was telling her that she was not at fault. He'd already been stalking Gage.

"Why?" she whispered.

"Francis and McClellan started off hot on your husband's trail. But then they began questioning whether he'd really killed that janitor. I needed to put them back on his case and give them a reason to blow him away."

The matter-of-fact way he said it sent a shiver over her skin. "Why did you kill the janitor?"

His eyes narrowed, and she couldn't stop

herself from cringing. "The same reason. To get the cops after him. What do you think? Once he escaped from the hospital, he was too dangerous to stay on the loose."

"Did Dr. Morton shoot at him? Or was it Hank Riddell, the man you assigned to watch Gage?"

"Gage and Wes." He gave her a smug look. "No, the shooter was me, actually. I happened to be on site, and I thought I could nip the problem in the bud. It would have been so much easier if I'd just shot your husband before he had a chance to get away."

She swallowed, wondering if she could get just a little more information out of Edmonston without getting hurt. He was obviously enjoying her interest. "How did you get away from a trained SWAT team at the estate?"

"I dressed like them. In the confusion, I pretended to be looking for you like everybody else. When I was out of sight, I got to my car and drove away."

When he smirked at her, she tried one more question: "That explosion. Were you working with an unstable chemical? Is that what happened?"

Edmonston's eyes narrowed. "We've wasted enough time. I don't have to tell you any more." He gave her a speculative look. "I presume your husband is worried sick about you, with the transmission cut off and all. You're going to call him on the phone and tell him you're still alive."

"Then what?"

"Tell him that if he wants to save your life, he'd better get over here as fast as he can."

"And walk into a trap?"

"You have a choice. I can start doing some things to you that will be very painful. Do you want to find out how much you can take before you make the call?"

Chapter Fifteen

"That won't be necessary." The comment came from behind Lily.

With a mixture of relief and fear, she whipped her head toward the doorway to see Gage, a gun in his hand.

Edmonston's reflexes were excellent. He dove behind the desk, firing as he dropped into a defensive crouch.

Gage ducked to the side of the doorway, cursing, and she knew he couldn't defend himself because she was in the way.

"Are you all right?" she shouted anxiously.

When he answered yes, she breathed a sigh of relief.

"Move where I can see you or I'll kill your wife," the Cranesbrook president growled.

Lily watched Gage's shoulders sag as he moved to the door again.

"Put your gun on the carpet."

Gage complied.

Cautiously, Edmonston slid his body along the back of the desk, then reached out a hand and pulled Lily's chair toward him, yanking her head around so she was staring into his angry eyes.

"How did he get here?" he growled.

She shrugged. "I guess he didn't trust me so he followed me to the campus."

She wasn't about to tell the truth—that she and Gage had worked out the scenario with the transmitter. They'd *wanted* Edmonston to find it, so he'd assume he'd destroyed Gage's ability to eavesdrop. Really, that transmitter had only been a decoy. She was wearing another, much smaller version that was hidden in the snap at the top of her slacks.

So there had never been a time when Gage hadn't been able to hear her conversation with Cranesbrook's president. They had his confession on tape. Now she just had to live long enough for it to do her any good.

She'd thought it was such a clever idea. She

hadn't been prepared to have Edmonston tie her in this chair, so she was stuck between him and Gage.

"What are you going to do?" she asked Edmonston.

His voice was cold as an ice storm. "Get out of here. With you as a shield."

She struggled to repress a hysterical laugh. Kidnapped again. Only this time it wasn't a man she knew wouldn't hurt her.

Edmonston shot a quick glance toward the door. Gage was no longer visible.

"Darnell," Edmonston shouted.

"Let her go."

"I will. After I get away."

Lily kept her lips pressed together because she knew that anything she said now would only be a distraction.

"If you hurt her, I'll kill you."

"Shut up and give me some maneuvering room. How much did you hear?"

"Enough."

"But it won't do you any good. Now back up."

Gage clenched his teeth and did as he was told. For just a moment, his eyes met Lily's. She knew he was trying to tell her something. But she didn't know what it was.

Edmonston divided his attention between her and the doorway. Quickly he untied the major knots that held her fast.

"Take off the rest of the rope," he ordered.

She did.

"Stand up."

Again, she complied. He came close to her, his voice low so that he thought she was the only one who could hear him. He didn't know about the transmitter on her pants. "We're going down the stairs, out the door and into my car. If you do anything to try and screw me up, you're dead. Understand?"

"Yes."

Edmonston stood behind her, poking her in the back with the gun. "Move."

She struggled to stay steady on her feet. As they stepped into the doorway, she saw Gage standing in the corner, his face grim.

Edmonston was behind her, but she could see his reflection in the glass door ahead of her.

He turned his head toward Gage. "Sit down."

Gage lowered himself to one of the chairs across from the receptionist's desk.

Edmonston raised his gun and pointed it at Gage. And she knew in that terrible moment that the man who held her captive had one final trick up his sleeve. He was going to shoot her husband.

"Get down," Gage shouted.

"No." She reared back and yanked at the man's arm. The gun discharged, but she'd thrown Edmonston's aim off, and the shot went wild, hitting the desk.

In the next moment, a bowl on the shelf across the room exploded in a shower of glass.

Edmonston whirled and fired at the bookcase.

Gage leaped forward, pulling Lily away from the executive.

As she hit the floor, Lily saw another man emerge from the closet in the corner of the room—Rand McClellan. He was holding a gun, and he pulled the trigger, once, twice.

Blood soaked the front of Edmonston's white shirt, and he went down.

McClellan rushed forward. Gun still drawn, he knelt over Edmonston.

"He's still alive," he muttered.

Speaking directly to the Cranesbrook executive, he said, "I'm Rand McClellan, and I vowed to bring down the man who killed my partner, Richard Francis. So, roast in hell."

Edmonston made a gurgling sound, then went still.

Rand felt for a pulse in his neck, then looked up. "He's dead," the detective said. "And the last thing he heard was my voice."

"I'm glad," Lily whispered.

Gage was still focused on the practical. "What kind of gun does he have?" he asked.

"A Sig P220 Sport."

"I think we can assume it was the murder weapon," Gage said.

"Even without the gun, we have enough to hang him," Rand said. "If he were still alive."

"So Gage is cleared," Lily said.

"He will be."

"Thank God," she breathed.

Gage took her in his arms. "You did it," he said, hugging her tightly.

Lily let him usher her away from the body and into Edmonston's office where she sagged onto the sofa. "Are you all right?" she gasped out.

"Yes. Are you?"

"Yes."

Gage kept his gaze squarely on her, his expression fierce. "Why the hell didn't you get down when I told you to drop?"

"He was going to shoot you."

"McClellan had him covered. But he couldn't shoot with you in the way. So I was going to provide a distraction."

"The bowl?"

"Yes."

"I'm sorry. All I could see was the gun pointed at you. And I couldn't ..." She tried to say more, then gave up.

The detective came to the doorway and looked over at Gage. "I'm going to call the department."

Gage nodded, but Lily couldn't let him go yet. "Tell me again. You know that Gage didn't kill anyone. Not that man at the hospital and not your partner."

"Yes."

"I'm so sorry about your partner," she said. "I wish it hadn't happened."

He gave a tight nod. "Thanks."

"So we're not under arrest," she clarified.

"Not for murder."

"For what?" she challenged.

"There's a little matter of some stolen cars." When he saw the look of anguish on her face, he went on rapidly. "But under the circumstances, I think I can get the D. A. to make a deal—if you two agree to stick around and help us with the case."

"Of course," Lily breathed.

"For starters, how do you think that glass bowl broke?"

"I don't know," she answered, keeping her gaze away from Gage so that she wouldn't give anything away.

GAGE GAVE his wife a long look. They had agreed in advance that they weren't going to talk about his special talent. Of course, that did leave some questions—like how he'd escaped from the hospital. But he was going to handle that part of the interrogation. All Lily had to do was tell what had happened to her.

The detective was speaking again. "It sounds like Dr. Morton wasn't a major player. I guess he was called in to deal with you when you went berserk. But we'll get a straight story out of him."

Rand looked at Gage speculatively. "What exactly did the chemical do to you?"

"First it made me sick to my stomach. Then it knocked me out and confused me." He shrugged. "And I guess it did make me a little aggressive. After that, I was woozy. But I don't know if it was from the chemical or from the stuff Morton gave me."

Rand nodded, still keeping his focus on Gage, looking as though he was evaluating his story.

Gage kept talking, "I gather Edmonston was counting on Morton keeping me in the hospital. Maybe he was going to visit me and slip me something fatal. But I escaped before he could do that." He gave the detective a long look. "Edmonston did a lot of killing in the past few weeks. I can't help wondering if there's more to the story than the cover-up of a lab accident. Like maybe there's something major going on at the lab that we still don't know about."

Rand nodded. "I intend to find out."

A SIREN SOUNDED outside, and Gage was glad that the interrogation was over for the moment.

When McClellan went to meet the team from the medical examiner's office, Gage wrapped his arms around Lily again and held on to her.

"You did great," he murmured.

"So did you."

"We've been through the hard part. This is just the cleanup now."

"I'm ready," she said. He knew she wished they

could just leave. But he also knew she'd come through on this phase, too. Because that was the kind of woman he'd married. Strong and steady. And unwilling to give up on her man, even when he'd been acting like a jerk.

Back at the State Police barracks, McClellan went pretty easy on them, mindful of what they'd been through. And since the detective didn't know about it, Gage didn't mention the money he'd taken from the ATMs. There was no way to tie those robberies to him, but he'd kept track of his illegal withdrawals, and he was going to pay the money back as soon as he could.

At one in the morning, when the interview session ended, Gage was feeling wrung out. And also a bit dazed. He'd been on the run for so long that it was still hard to grasp that he wasn't a murder suspect anymore.

And although he and McClellan had been adversaries for the past few weeks, he had decided that the detective wasn't such a bad guy, especially when he offered to give them a ride.

"To the beach house we, uh, borrowed?" Lily asked as they stood in the lobby of the police barracks. "We can pay the weekly rent. Then we'll be legal on that."

Gage cut in. "We'll go there later and pick up our stuff. I've arranged something else."

"When?"

"I made a phone call when you were being interviewed." He glanced at McClellan.

"I've already got the address," the detective said.

He drove them to a very upscale inn that Gage had passed many times on the way to St. Stephens from Baltimore. He knew it was expensive, but he wanted to take Lily somewhere they could celebrate. After that, he'd make it a priority to find out what had happened to his partner, Bray.

When they got out, he and the detective shook hands. "I'm sorry about your partner," he said.

"He was a good guy. But we got the bastard who killed him."

"You thought I was that bastard," Gage said.

"I'm glad you're not."

Lily also shook the man's hand. "I think you're letting us off easy," she murmured.

"It's the least I can do after hunting you down like rabid dogs."

Gage laughed. "Yeah."

The cop climbed back into his unmarked, and Gage escorted Lily into the elegantly decorated lobby.

"Mr. and Mrs. Smith?" the desk asked.

"Right," Gage answered. When Lily gave him a questioning look, he gave a small shake of his head.

He signed them in and paid cash for the room, then took his wife up to their luxury room on the second floor.

"Mr. and Mrs. Smith," she said. "And no luggage. He probably assumes we're cheating on our spouses."

"Better than thinking we're murderers. Until the news hits tomorrow, we need to keep a low profile. And after that, too, if we don't want every reporter who's been covering the story descending on us."

She laughed nervously. "Right."

"But maybe we can sell our story to one of those supermarket tabloids."

"You mean the ones with stories about alien abductions and space cats?"

"Yeah."

She squeezed Gage's hand, marveling at how much his mood had changed since they'd left the State Police barracks.

Still holding on to him, she turned to look at their surroundings. The bedroom was elegantly furnished in the colonial style, with a king-size bed, a spacious sitting area and a bathroom with a spa tub and separate shower.

Gage had ordered a bottle of champagne, which sat in an ice bucket across from the bed. He eased out the cork, poured two flutes and handed one to Lily. "To us," he murmured.

They clinked glasses, and each took a sip.

"I can't believe it's over," she whispered. "I can't believe we're not on the run."

"Well, I agreed to get the undamaged vehicles back to their owners and pay for the one that got riddled with bullet holes."

"Uh, you didn't mention a car that was riddled with bullet holes."

He made a face. "Damn. I must be too tired to think about what I'm saying."

"Tell me about the bullet holes," she insisted.

"That was when I tried to break into Cranesbrook. The security guys gave chase with guns blazing."

"I thought there was more to the story than you'd told me."

"A little. And by the way, I didn't mention to McClellan the part about the money I stole. What he doesn't know won't hurt him. And I'll pay it all back."

"I know you will."

He reached for her glass and set it down on the dresser along with his, then pulled her to him and hugged her tight.

"What happens now?" she whispered.

"What do you want to happen?"

She made a small sound.

"What?"

"I was thinking that I don't have a job. And Five Star can't be in good financial shape. What are we going to live on, exactly?"

"Before this incident, I had a company interested in buying my miniaturized transmitter when I perfected it. I'd say we conducted the definitive test tonight."

She nodded.

"It's worth a lot. I should be able to get a quick down payment and the rest later."

She nuzzled her lips against his cheek. "Your hard work paid off."

"Tomorrow I have to contact Peggy Olson and tell her I'm back."

"Yes."

"While we're making plans…" He trailed off because they really hadn't discussed the next part. At least not recently.

"What?"

"I was going to say you don't have to look for another job if you want to stay home and have a baby."

Her eyes glowed. "You want to have a baby?"

"There's nothing like running for your life to make you think about what's really important. Home and family," he said with a hitch in his voice.

"Oh, Gage." She hugged him to her, then pulled back so she could meet his eyes. "What about your new talent? How does that fit in?"

"It sure came in handy for escaping from the police."

"Yes."

"But I honestly don't know what I do with it now. Or how long it'll last." He felt his expression turn serious. "Is it a problem for you? Having a husband who can do weird stuff?"

"No. Nothing is a problem, as long as we make our marriage work. As long as we don't turn away from each other ever again."

"Never again," he said, meaning it from the bottom of his heart.

She relaxed against him, and he smiled to himself as a very enticing idea took hold. He dipped his head, bringing his lips to Lily's. The kiss was a declaration of his love, of his commitment. And he felt the same commitment from her. He angled her body, stroking her breast with one hand, combing his fingers through her hair with the other. And then he used a third hand—the one that existed only in his mind—to cup her bottom and bring her hips more tightly against his.

It took a moment for her to realize what he was doing. When she did, she pulled back and looked at him in shock. "Gage?"

He grinned. "That's one good use for my talent, don't you think?"

Then he brought his lips back to hers, telling her wordlessly what he intended for the future.

* * * * *

Look for the next title in the
SECURITY BREACH *trilogy next month.*
CRITICAL EXPOSURE
by Ann Voss Peterson.

A special treat for you from Harlequin Blaze!

Turn the page for a sneak preview of
DECADENT
by
New York Times *bestselling author*
Suzanne Forster

Available November 2006,
wherever series books are sold.

Harlequin Blaze—Your ultimate destination
for red-hot reads.
With six titles every month, you'll never guess
what you'll discover under the covers...

whispers. But Ally had never put much stock
the fantasy. She didn't believe in ghosts.

RUN, ALLY! Don't be fooled by him. He's evil. Don't let him touch you!

But as the forbidding figure came through the mists toward her, Ally knew she couldn't run. His features burned with dark malevolence, and his physical domination of everything around him seemed to hold her like a net.

She'd heard the tales. She knew all about the Wolverton legend and the ghost that haunted The Willows, an elegant old mansion lost by Micha Wolverton nearly a hundred years ago. According to folklore, the estate was stolen from the Wolvertons, and Micha was killed, trying to reclaim it. His dying vow was to be reunited with the spirit of his beloved wife, who'd taken her life for reasons no one would speak of, except in whispers. But Ally had never put much stock in the fantasy. She didn't believe in ghosts.

Until now—

She still didn't understand what was happening. The figure had materialized out of the mist that lay thick on the damp cemetery soil. A cool breeze and silvery moonlight had played against the ancient stone of the crypts surrounding her, until they joined the mist, causing his body to thicken and solidify right before her eyes. That was when she realized she'd seen this man before. Or thought she had, at least.

His face was familiar...so familiar, yet she couldn't put it together. Not with him looming so near. She stepped back as he approached.

"Don't be afraid," he said. His voice wasn't what she expected. It didn't sound as if it were coming from beyond the grave. It was deep and sensual. Commanding.

"Who are you?" she managed.

"You should know. You summoned me."

"No, I didn't." She had no idea what he was talking about. Two minutes ago, she'd been crouching behind a moss-covered crypt, spying on the mansion that had once been The Willows, but was now Club Casablanca. And then this—

If he was Micha, he might be angry that she was trespassing on his property. "I'll go," she said. "I won't come back. I promise."

"You're not going anywhere."

Words snagged in her throat. "Wh-why not? What do you want?"

"If I wanted something, Ally, I'd take it. This is about need."

His words resonated as he moved within inches of her. She tried to back away, but her feet were useless. "And you need something from me?"

"Good guess." His tone burned with irony. "I need lips, soft and surrendered, a body limp with desire."

"My lips, my bod—?"

"Only yours."

"Why? Why me?" This couldn't be Micha. He didn't want any woman but Rose. He'd died trying to get back to her.

"Because you want that, too," he said.

Wanted what? A ghost of her own? She'd always found the legend impossibly romantic, but how could he have known that? How could he know anything about her? Besides, she'd sworn off inappropriate men, and what could be more inappropriate than a ghost? She shook her head again, still not willing to admit the truth. But her heart wouldn't play along. It clattered inside her chest. The mere thought of his kiss, his touch, terrified her. This wildness, it was fear, wasn't it?

When his fingertips touched her cheek, she

flinched, expecting his flesh to be cold, lifeless. It was anything but that. His skin was smooth and hot, gentle, yet demanding. And while his dark brown eyes were filled with mystery and wonder, there was a sensitivity about them that threatened to disarm her if she looked too deeply.

"These lips are mine," he said, as if stating a universal fact that she was helpless to avoid. In truth, it was just that. She couldn't stop him.

And she didn't want to.

* * * * *

Find out how the story unfolds in...
DECADENT
by New York Times *bestselling author*
Suzanne Forster.
On sale November 2006.
Harlequin Blaze—Your ultimate destination
for red-hot reads.
With six titles every month, you'll never guess
what you'll discover under the covers...

◆ HARLEQUIN®

Live the emotion™

American ROMANCE®

Heart, Home & Happiness

◆ HARLEQUIN®

Blaze™

Red-hot reads.

Harlequin® Historical
Historical Romantic Adventure!

◆ HARLEQUIN®

HARLEQUIN ROMANCE®

From the Heart, For the Heart

◆ HARLEQUIN®

INTRIGUE®

Breathtaking Romantic Suspense

Medical Romance™...
love is just a heartbeat away

Ne xt™

**There's the life you planned.
And there's what comes next.**

◆ HARLEQUIN®

Presents

Seduction and Passion Guaranteed!

◆ HARLEQUIN®

Super Romance®

Exciting, Emotional, Unexpected

www.eHarlequin.com

HDIR106

HARLEQUIN ROMANCE®

The rush of falling in love,

Cosmopolitan,
international settings,

Believable, feel-good stories
about today's women

The compelling thrill
of romantic excitement

It could happen to you!

EXPERIENCE
HARLEQUIN ROMANCE!

Available wherever Harlequin Books are sold.

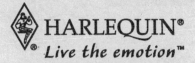

HARLEQUIN®
Live the emotion™

www.eHarlequin.com

HROMDIR04

HARLEQUIN®

American ROMANCE®

Invites *you* to experience lively, heartwarming all-American romances

Every month, we bring you four strong, sexy men, and four women who know what they want—and go all out to get it.

From small towns to big cities, experience a sense of adventure, romance and family spirit—the all-American way!

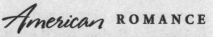
American ROMANCE

Heart, Home & Happiness

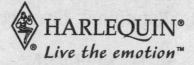
HARLEQUIN®
Live the emotion™

www.eHarlequin.com   HARDIR06

HARLEQUIN®

Super Romance®

...there's more to the story!

Superromance.
A *big* satisfying read about unforgettable
characters. Each month we offer *six* very different
stories that range from family drama to adventure
and mystery, from highly emotional stories to
romantic comedies—and much more! Stories
about people you'll believe in and care about.
Stories too compelling to put down....

Our authors are among today's *best* romance
writers. You'll find familiar names and talented
newcomers. Many of them are award winners—
and you'll see why!

If you want the biggest and best
in romance fiction, you'll get it
from Superromance!

Exciting, Emotional, Unexpected...

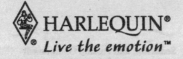

HARLEQUIN®
Live the emotion™

www.eHarlequin.com   HSDIR06

HARLEQUIN®
Presents

The world's bestselling romance series...
The series that brings you your favorite authors,
month after month:

Helen Bianchin...Emma Darcy
Lynne Graham...Penny Jordan
Miranda Lee...Sandra Marton
Anne Mather...Carole Mortimer
Susan Napier...Michelle Reid

and many more uniquely talented authors!

Wealthy, powerful, gorgeous men...
Women who have feelings just like your own...
The stories you love, set in exotic, glamorous locations...

HARLEQUIN®
Presents

Seduction and Passion Guaranteed!

www.eHarlequin.com   HPDIR104

Harlequin® Historical
Historical Romantic Adventure!

*Imagine a time of chivalrous
knights and unconventional ladies,
roguish rakes and impetuous
heiresses, rugged cowboys
and spirited frontierswomen—
these rich and vivid tales will
capture your imagination!*

*Harlequin Historical...
they're too good to miss!*